'I think I [...] repay you[...]'

It suddenly occurred to Logan that she was about to make him an offer he couldn't refuse. 'Like a barter?'

'Yes,' Paige said nervously. ' I want you to know up front that you're not, uh…obliged to do it.'

Logan got up and walked towards her. 'Now, why,' he said softly, 'would you think I'd say no to such a proposition?'

'Well, b-because you haven't heard…all the…' Her breath caught when he traced the curve of her jaw with his finger. '…particulars.'

'I've heard it called a lot of things, but *never* that.' He leaned forward, nuzzling her neck. 'So, when did you want to consummate this barter?'

'You're talking about…you think I'm offering …myself?' Paige asked, pulling away from him. She reached into her pocket, pulled out a diamond bracelet and slammed it on the counter. 'That's what I'm offering. And I can guarantee it's worth several times what I owe.'

Logan stared at the piece of jewellery. Damn. He was thinking hot sex and she offered cold rocks. *So much for wish fulfilment…*

Dear Reader,

There's something about a motorcycle that's always caught my fancy. Maybe it's because the men that ride those powerful machines are the closest we come these days to a knight on a charging steed. Of course, the fact that my husband rides a beautiful touring bike might have something to do with it. Still, I've always wanted to write about a man, a motorcycle and a lady in need of rescue. The result is *Unlikely Hero*.

Cruising along a Texas highway on his Harley, Logan Walker doesn't have a care in the world until he spots a woman, stranded, trying to deal with two unsavoury characters. But he doesn't know what he's getting into, because from the minute he rescues Paige Davenport, she's nothing but gorgeous, tempting trouble.

So come along and meet this heartthrob. Logan is an unlikely hero, but I think you'll agree with Paige when she decides to hang on to him because 'There aren't enough heroes to go around these days.'

Happy Reading,

Sandy Steen

UNLIKELY HERO

by

Sandy Steen

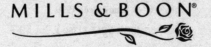

MILLS & BOON®

For Uncle Clifton,
my unlikely hero.
I miss you.

*MILLS & BOON and MILLS & BOON with the Rose Device
are registered trademarks of the publisher.
TEMPTATION is a registered trademark of
Harlequin Enterprises Limited, used under licence.*

*First published in Great Britain 2000
by Harlequin Mills & Boon Limited,
Eton House, 18-24 Paradise Road, Richmond, Surrey TW9 1SR*

© Sandy Steen 1999

ISBN 0 263 82360 1

21-0001

*Printed and bound in Spain
by Litografia Rosés S.A., Barcelona*

Prologue

HE WAS GETTING the hell out of Denver and it felt good. Good? It felt like he'd been let out of jail. After eight months of demanding cases and three aborted attempts at a well-earned vacation, Logan Walker was a man possessed. He was leaving town and nothing short of the Second Coming was going to stop him.

The phone rang.

Tuning out the persistent ringing, he grabbed a small duffel bag and began stuffing clothes into it. "Let the machine get it," he mumbled, squelching the urge to reach for the phone. It did, and a few seconds later he heard his partner's voice.

"Tex, you there?"

Logan snatched up the cordless receiver, cradled it between his shoulder and chin and shut off the answering machine. "If you're calling about a case, I'm already gone," he said, and went right on packing.

Rick Conner laughed. "Would I do that to you?"

"In a heartbeat. Don't forget, I've only had six hours of sleep after going without for almost thirty. I'm short on patience, so this better be a goodbye-and-have-a-great-time call."

"Oh, it is. It is."

"Uh-huh. Don't ever try to con another P.I., Rick."

"Busted, huh? All right, but we had an interesting call this morning and I thought we'd talk it over."

"I'm all talked out."

"Sure you don't want the details? This could get our name in the paper again."

"I haven't even read a newspaper in over three days. I couldn't care less."

"Okay, okay. But I still don't understand why you have to take off a whole month."

"Because I need to. For the next month I don't even want to think about being a private investigator. The only thing I wanna be suspicious of is whether or not the local bar may run out of beer. And the only surveillance I wanna participate in is seeing which Lone Star lovely has the longest legs. Besides, it's time you stood alone, partner."

"Well, can't say I haven't learned from the best. Did I ever tell you how much I appreciate you taking me on as a partner, teaching me everything—"

"Stuff it, Conner. You must be slipping with all that flattery."

"Hey, cut me some slack. This is my first solo."

"You'll be fine, and I'll be better—just as soon as I see the Sweetwater Springs city-limits sign."

"I don't see why you feel you have to go to Texas to have a good time."

"You wouldn't unless you're from Texas." He'd deliberately failed to mention that his fifteen-year high-school reunion was scheduled for the following weekend. Even though he was going home, Logan still wasn't sure he was going to the festivities, and he damned sure didn't need Rick teasing him about it.

"Say, you wouldn't have a woman stashed away down there that I don't know about, would you?"

"Nope." For the first time in a long time he wished that were true. He had to admit walking into the reunion dance with a tall, leggy blonde on his arm would make going a lot more appealing.

"I was afraid of that. You know, you might think about looking up some old friends while you're there. Like maybe a high-school sweetheart or—"

"What is it with you newly married men? You just can't stand to see a single guy running around loose, or what?"

"You're my partner. I want you to find a good woman and be happy."

"I don't want a good woman. Now, a bad one on the other hand—"

"Talk's cheap. Come to think of it, I don't know what I'm worried about. Workaholics don't have time for romance. You won't last a week."

"The hell I won't. No more whiny husbands looking for a runaway wife. No more wives trying to catch hubby being unfaithful so they can take him for all he's worth."

"What about cases like that little Wilson girl?

You found her, Logan, when almost everybody else had given up."

"And wound up with reporters doggin' my steps for a week. Every time I poked my head out of the door one of them wanted a quote. Wish I'd just kept my nose out of the whole thing."

"But you didn't. And that's what I'm saying. You can't walk away from a puzzle until you solve it, or a cry for help until you answer it."

Cases like finding a five-year-old girl abducted by a mentally unstable nanny made all the boring, mundane work bearable. But those cases were few and far between, which made it even more important that he take this time off. He needed to recharge his batteries. And, by heaven, have some fun.

"Besides," Rick continued, "our phone hasn't stopped ringing since the Wilson case. It didn't hurt a bit that Andrew Wilson III is worth several million dollars and praised us to his wealthy friends. A bunch of the calls are from some very rich people. They think we're—excuse me—you're the best, and they won't settle for anything less. And be grateful they're calling or you wouldn't be able to take this little sabbatical."

"All right, I've had my fifteen minutes of fame. It's your job to save the world for the next month."

"Have it your way, Tex, but my money's on human nature. Your nature. And it doesn't make any difference if you're in Denver, Sweetwater Springs or the North Pole, the first beady-eyed character or damsel in distress you run across

will pique your curiosity and that's all it will
take. No matter how much you protest that you
want to be left alone, you're a sucker for trouble.''

Logan stuffed the last of his clothes into the
bag. "Don't bet on it. Except for one last bag I'm
packing even as we speak, the bike is loaded and
I'm ready to roll. In an hour I'll be on the open
road with nothing ahead of me but good friends
and good times. I could stumble across a serial
killer or the sexiest woman alive and wouldn't
even give them a second glance. So long, partner,
it's all yours.'' And he hung up before Rick could
elaborate on another of his character flaws.

Logan zipped the duffel bag closed, grabbed
his helmet and weathered leather bomber jacket
and locked the door behind him. He didn't look
back.

1

FOR THE FIRST time in her life, Paige Davenport felt free. Totally, wonderfully free. Breezing along Highway 87 headed for Houston, Texas, savoring the sweet taste of freedom on a warm May afternoon, she didn't have a care in the world.

Until the borrowed Jaguar XJS sports car she was driving belched and shuddered simultaneously.

A few seconds later it happened again, only this time she felt the shudder right through the steering wheel. Lord, what was that? Except for occasionally pumping her own gas, the total sum of her knowledge of cars could be inscribed on the head of a pin. But even she knew that wasn't the way a car was supposed to sound or act.

Then came a kind of clunking sound. Actually it was more like clunka-de-clunka, but by that time Paige realized descriptions were immaterial. And the smoke billowing out from under the hood of the little forest-green car confirmed it. As the car rolled to a stop on the side of the highway near a sign that warned Don't Mess With Texas, she knew she was in trouble. Big trouble.

Now what?

Trying not to remember all the horror stories and warnings about women traveling alone, she fought a creeping panic. She had her cell phone, of course, but didn't want to use it. It could be used to track her down. No, the phone was for a dire emergency, life-or-death situation.

Paige glanced back in the direction of the last town, Clayton, New Mexico. The map indicated nine miles between Clayton and Texline, Texas, and she estimated she was about halfway. Four plus miles of practically deserted highway in either direction. So deserted, in fact, she recalled seeing only one vehicle, an eighteen-wheeler she'd passed as she drove out of Clayton. She could be stranded here for hours before another car came along. Even then, there was no guarantee a driver would stop and help. She racked her brain trying to remember if Texas had enacted a "Good Samaritan" law, but couldn't. Although, to be honest, if there was such a law, there wasn't anything she could do if someone decided to ignore the law and her. It wasn't as if she could get a license number and report them to the authorities. The last thing Paige wanted was to be involved with the law.

"So," she threw her hands up in frustration, saying aloud, "this is what comes of allowing my emotions to run amuck and overrule my common sense."

As soon as the words were out of her mouth she regretted them. Not because they weren't essentially true, but because they were precisely the words her mother would have said, probably was saying about Paige. A mental image of her impeccably dressed mother pacing back and forth in what had always been referred to as the family room flashed through her mind. Family room. What a joke. The Davenports were a lineage, not a family. And if she knew her mother, Kat Davenport was probably doing more than pacing. She was probably making the lives of everyone around her miserable while trying to find her less-than-dutiful child. Not to mention frantically attempting to contain the scandal.

Ah, yes, the scandal. A blemish on the Davenport name.

The unforgivable sin.

Paige had been raised on that doctrine, chapter and verse. Not that her childhood was unhappy, but definitely formal, with an emphasis on who she was rather than what she dreamed of becoming. Her parents made little effort to understand her need to create, to take a blank sketch pad or canvas and transform it into something unique and wonderful. Being an artist was fine as a hobby, but not as a career. Even the meager salary Paige earned teaching art to underprivileged children wasn't considered anything other than charity work. The fact that she wanted to continue to teach, maybe even start her own school, was laudable but unrealistic as far as her family was concerned. It was selfish, her mother had always insisted, to put her wants and needs ahead of what was best for the family. She was, after all, a Davenport.

God, how Paige hated those words. Her mother's words. The credo she was expected to live by.

In retrospect it was easy to see how the slow, but steady indoctrination of that credo had brought her to this moment. Worse, she could see how she had gradually given up even her small attempts to break free of the velvet-lined Davenport shackles. Over the years, each rebellion had ended with her mother persuading her that as an only child she was obligated to take her proper place in Denver society, including marrying the right man. By the time she was an adult she had become so indoctrinated that she didn't even realize how confining those shackles had become. Looking back, to her horror, Paige realized she had become a clone of her mother.

But walking into her fiancé's apartment last night had changed everything.

Knowing how much Kat Davenport loved to control every situation, Paige smiled thinking of the stunned expression that must have been on her mother's face this morning when she learned her daughter, heiress to millions and a lofty perch on the Denver social ladder, had walked, no, run, from all of it without a backward glance. The only thing more fascinating would have been watching her fiancé, Randal the Rat, try to justify his behavior to her mother. Just how did a man explain to his almost mother-in-law that the bride had accidentally walked in on a teeny-tiny indiscretion?

Like having wild sex with one of her brides-maids right after the rehearsal dinner.

Indiscretion. That's what her mother had called it last night when Paige raced into the house in tears and told her what happened. Not an insult, or even an affront. And indiscretions, according to Kat, could be overlooked. The situation was salvageable if only Paige would be realistic. "Wild oats and that sort of thing." The shock of walking in on Randal paled in comparison to the pain of hearing her mother so easily dismiss what had happened. So easily dismiss her feelings.

But that pain had been her wake-up call.

In those few moments she'd made a decision based not on logic or even right or wrong. Something, some instinct she wasn't even aware of until that moment, told her that if she stayed another hour, another minute, she might be lost forever. This might be her last chance.

So she ran.

Leaving her mother in midlecture, Paige had walked out of the house and driven straight to the home of the only person she could call a true friend, Regina Fox.

A free-spirited, endearing eccentric, Regi adored two pastimes: traveling and thumbing her nose at "polite society." And she had enough money to do both whenever she wanted. Her bank account more than equaled the Davenports, but she had something they didn't. Guts.

God bless Regi. They had talked into the night. Not just about what had happened, but about what Paige really wanted out of life. The strange part was no one had ever asked her what she wanted. She didn't even remember Randal ever actually asking her to marry him. They had known each other since childhood, they went to the same schools, traveled in the same circles.

Everyone, including Paige, expected them to marry. And when she'd found him with another woman she'd been shocked. But after pouring her heart out to Regi she'd discovered what she hadn't been.

Heartbroken.

Her heart should have been shattered into tiny pieces at the thought of the man she was supposed to marry in bed with someone else, much less actually experiencing it. It should have been. But it wasn't. In fact, she'd been much more upset by the betrayal of her bridesmaid, a so-called friend who, Paige now realized, she'd only asked to stand up with her because her parents approved of her. She now knew a cold hard fact.

She didn't love Randal.

Not the way a woman was supposed to love a man. She never had. And that realization, even more than her mother's reaction, made her see herself and her life in a harshly revealing light. Not a pretty picture.

When had she stopped being an individual and become merely "a Davenport"? When had she lost her dreams? Asking the questions helped move her past the hurt to a healthy anger. Once there, Paige didn't want to let go. The anger cleansed and clarified. She had some choices to make and she made them. She knew what she wanted out of life. "Life, liberty and the pursuit of happiness" ceased to be a phrase from the Constitution and became her anthem.

Only too happy to give aid and comfort to the escapee, including loaning some money, Regi set up a job interview with a friend who owned an art gallery in Houston. Then, since she was leaving for Europe within hours, she traded cars with Paige, hugged her goodbye and pointed her in the direction of Texas. And now, for the first time in more of her twenty-seven years than Paige cared to remember, she was seeing life from a different perspective. Without Davenport money and influence. But most of all, without Davenport control.

She was free.

Free to live her own life without always stopping to consider if what she said or did was PDC. Politically Davenport Correct. Paige thought if she had a nickel for every time she was cautioned to "remember you're a Davenport," she'd be independently wealthy herself.

Come to think of it, she owed Randal the Rat a big fat thank-you. If she hadn't found him with one of her best friends she might never have had the courage to break free of family pressures. Of course, eventually there would be a price to pay. There always was. And there was no doubt her mother already had one or more private detectives working twenty-four hours a day trying to find her. Discreetly, of course. Particularly given the well-constructed cover story—a ruptured appendix. Very severe case, the morning newspaper had reported, but Miss Davenport was recuperating quietly in a private hospital. Un-doubtedly, there was an empty room in some hospital with her name and a No Visitors sign on the door. Her mother was a master at covering all the bases.

But this time there would be no going back.

This time Paige was determined to be free and stay free. Once she had a job and her own income, and some distance from Denver, she knew she could find her own life. And she hadn't deluded herself that her new life would be easy, or that there wouldn't be times when she would long for just a few of the luxuries she'd always taken for granted. Unlike her mother, she didn't expect perfection. Maybe it was silly for a grown woman to run away from home, but Paige knew it was the only way she would be able to stand on her own feet. And in order to do that, she needed time and anonymity. Mostly anonymity.

She glanced back at the stretch of still-deserted highway she'd just covered. Well, if it was time she wanted, it appeared she had it in spades. Then she looked down the long road ahead and she thought she saw the outline of a vehicle on the horizon. Was that a car? *Oh, please, let it be a car.*

It was a truck, but to Paige it looked like a golden chariot. She scrambled out of the Jaguar waving her arms and almost cried with relief when she saw the truck pull off on her side of the road and stop. Two men, one tall and slim, the other short and stocky, got out of the truck.

The slim man pushed his straw cowboy hat back on his head and grinned. "What's the problem, little lady?"

Little lady? If she hadn't been so thrilled they'd stopped to help, she might have been offended. "I don't know. The, uh, the car made a funny noise then smoke started coming out from beneath the hood."

"Well, now, let's just take a look-see." The slim man motioned to his friend now on the other side of her car. Stocky opened the door, sat down in the passenger seat then leaned over and pulled on something. The car's hood popped up slightly.

"I can't tell you how grateful I am that you stopped. I thought it might be hours before I saw another human," Paige said as he raised the hood and peered at the motor. "I'm afraid I don't know anything about cars and this one isn't even mine. I borrowed it from a friend."

"That so?" he said without looking up.

"Yes, I—" The slamming of the hood cut her off.

"Well, I'm no mechanic, but looks like you busted a fan belt." He held up a narrow band of rubber frayed almost in two in one spot.

"Is that bad?"

He whipped a knife from his pocket and with the touch of a button the blade sprang out, slicing through the remainder of the fan belt as if it were tissue paper. "Bad enough, I reckon." Slim's grin altered, sliding into something that looked more like a leer. His gaze slithered over Paige making the hair on the back of her neck stand up. Suddenly she wanted them to leave. Suddenly stranded and alone looked better to her than the glint in Slim's eyes. "Can't be fixed out here."

"Are you sure? I mean—"

"You callin' my friend a liar?"

Paige spun around, backing up against the car. While she had been focused on the man checking under the hood of car, his companion had crept up behind her. "No. No, I didn't mean to insinuate anything of the kind."

Slim moved closer. "I reckon you better ride into town with us."

"Yeah," his friend said. "Got some cold beer in the truck. How 'bout it?"

Dear God!

In the middle of nowhere, with not another human being in sight, the gravity of the situation hit Paige with gale wind force. With her back to the car and a man on each side of her, she was trapped. What a fool she'd been. So grateful for the offer of help, she hadn't stopped to consider their motives might be less than pure. Her only hope lay in the cell phone in the glove compartment of the car. And this definitely was a dire emergency. Maybe even a life-or-death situation. Slowly she inched her left hand toward the handle. If she could move fast enough…

The roar of a motorcycle engine approaching from the north sounded like an angels' chorus to Paige's ears.

"Someone's comin'. What if he stops?" the stocky man asked.

"Shut up. Just look like you're helpin' fix a flat tire and he'll go on by." Slim grabbed Paige's arm and lay the blade of his knife between her shoulder blades. "No callin' out or tryin' to signal, you hear?"

Paige nodded, praying the rider would stop, even if he turned out to be one of those Hell's Angels she'd read about. Anything was better than what she feared Slim and his friend had in

store for her. Slim moved closer. While Stocky
opened the trunk and took out a jack, Paige tried
to think. She had to stop the rider. He might be
her only hope. She was even prepared to throw
herself in front of the bike to insure he would
stop, if she could get free. Her heart racing, she
poised to dash into the road. *Please stop! Please
help me!* The roar of the motorcycle came closer,
closer.

Cruising southeast along Highway 87, Logan
spotted the little forest-green Jaguar sports car
from a half mile away. Then he saw the truck,
two men and a woman with red hair. Probably
car trouble. But were the men offering help or
were the two vehicles traveling together? Maybe
he should stop and lend a hand…

What was he doing? Before he even got a good
look at the situation he was already preparing to
step in when it might not even be necessary. Rick
was right, he thought. The first sign of a possible
damsel in distress and he was ready to jump to
the rescue. A knight in rusty armor. Not today,
Logan decided. He'd size up the situation as he
rode by, but that was road courtesy, nothing
more. He was too tired for anything else and had
no intention of stopping.

And he wouldn't have if he hadn't seen fear in
the woman's eyes when he rode past. Real fear,
and something else he thought looked like desperation. Logan hit the brakes, turned around
and pulled the bike to a stop on the opposite side
of the road from the car. He climbed off the sleek
black Harley-Davidson motorcycle, removed his
helmet and hung it on one of the handlebars.

Standing relaxed, his body language nonthreatening, he kept to his side of the road.

Logan nodded to the woman. "Afternoon, ma'am," he said in an easy drawl.

Wild-eyed, the trembling half-hearted smile she offered was as effective as a scream. He was betting these jokers were interested in money and sex, but hopefully not enough to face him down for it. "You boys need some help?"

"Naw," Slim said. "Just fixin' a flat."

Stocky stepped back from the open trunk. "That's right."

"Y'all traveling together?"

"Just stopped to help out the lady."

"Well, I guess you don't need me then."

"Nope, but 'preciate the offer," Slim told him.

"Wait!" the woman called out when Logan started to go.

"Yes ma'am?"

"I…I, uh, thanks for stopping."

"No sweat," he told her and smiled. "Y'all take it easy."

"Same goes," Slim called out.

Still smiling, Logan turned toward the motorcycle, reaching inside his jacket for his Glock at the same time. Before either of the other men knew what was happening he swung back around…his gun in hand.

"Now I don't know what's going on here, but there's no doubt in my mind this lady is scared. Right or wrong, ma'am?"

"R-right."

His gaze drilled Slim. "Then turn her loose."

Slim was so startled, he did exactly that.

Paige was equally startled, but she recovered in time to seize her opportunity to escape, racing across the road to the man with the gun. "You okay?" he asked without taking his eyes from the men.

"Y-yes. Thank goodness you came along when you did."

"Okay, boys. Here's how it plays out. Get in your truck—" he motioned with the gun "—and get the hell out of here. Now."

He didn't need to repeat himself.

Slim and Stocky couldn't scramble into the pickup fast enough, and their tires spit gravel as they took off headed north.

Logan committed the license plate to memory for future reference, then waited until the truck was almost out of sight before turning to the woman.

"Thank you," Paige said. "Thank you, thank you, thank you. I don't know what might have happened if you hadn't come along."

"I do."

Paige glanced at the gun in his hand. Oh, God had she gone from bad to worse? From a knife to a gun? "I—I…"

"Relax." He flicked the safety back on the gun and tucked it into his jacket. "I'm not after your body or your money. And I have a permit to carry a gun."

Relief shuddered through her. "Thanks."

"Don't you watch the evening news?"

"Excuse me?"

"A woman alone on the highway is an easy target."

"Well, I—"

"Damned careless, if you ask me."

"I beg your pardon." She knew she'd had a close call due to her own carelessness, but she'd be damned if she'd give him the satisfaction of hearing her admit it. He may have rescued her, but that didn't give him the right to be arrogant and rude. "I'm eternally grateful for what you did, Mr.—"

"Walker. Logan Walker."

"Well, Mr. Walker, I am grateful, but that doesn't give you the right to insult me. For your information, not every woman has a Sir Galahad waiting in the wings, or wants one for that matter. Some of us actually want to take care of ourselves."

"Whoa, Red." He held up both hands. "I'm not lookin' for a fight. You just have the look, as my grandmother used to say, of a woman who's been well kept. Not a whole lot of experience taking care of yourself, Miss…"

"D…uh, oh…" She gave him the first name that popped into her head. "O…O'Neil. Paige O'Neil. And what makes you think I haven't?"

Logan gave her a very slow once-over and had to admit it was no hardship. She had one of those flawless faces, and body that was easy on the eyes. Cheekbones any model would kill for, skin that begged to be touched and thick, rusty-red hair that fell past her shoulders. Aristocratic with the bearing to match. Probably from generations of wealth and good breeding. American royalty, he thought. Yeah, an untitled duchess if ever he saw one. From the top of her designer salon cut-

and-styled hair to the tips of her shoes that looked as if they could easily have cost half of what he paid for a month's rent, she looked like old money.

And trouble. Gorgeous, tempting trouble.

"Well, for one thing, you're dressed like you just left Saks Fifth Avenue after a round of serious shopping. Your jewelry looks real, especially those diamond studs in your ears. If not, it's damned expensive costume. Either way, you've got on just enough to be tempting. As for the car... Well, you don't have to be a rocket scientist to figure that little chunk of metal probably costs more to own and operate than most folks in this part of the state make in a year." He gave her a slow smile. "Probably don't even pump your own gas. And I'd bet you didn't even have the car checked out before you hit the road." He shook his head as if answering his own question. "No offense, ma'am, but you might as well be wearing a sign that says, Rob Me."

Paige started to give him a piece of her mind, then decided against it. The man was infuriatingly accurate, but he was now her only hope of getting help. And he had given her a new worry. If she was so transparent that this man could label her so quickly, what chance did she have of making it to Houston without some reporter, or the private bloodhounds she knew were already on her trail, doing the same? "I, uh, see your point. Sorry, I didn't mean to snap at you."

"Adrenaline. It'll wear off in a minute or two."

"Are you always so observant?"

"Usually. Noticed the fear in your eyes. That's what made me stop."

"And you knew just by looking at me and those men what was going on?"

"Old habit, I guess. I used to be a cop."

Paige's still-racing heartbeat jumped even faster. "Used to be?"

"Yeah, I quit about five years ago. Got tired of the bad guys getting off nine times out of ten."

Of all the people to stop and help, she had to end up with an ex-cop! Careful, she warned herself. He was probably sharp enough to see through even an experienced liar. He could be a dangerous complication. She had to be very careful about everything she said and decided staying as close to the truth as possible was her best bet of avoiding detection until she could part company with Logan Walker.

"I, uh, think you're right about the adrenaline. And the car, too. I should've had it serviced before I left, but it's not mine. I'm on my way to a job interview in Houston." That much, at least, was the truth.

"You got a pair of jeans, Duchess?"

"Certainly—what did you call me?"

"Never mind."

"I fail to see why my wardrobe is any of your business."

"Just answer the question. Do you, or don't you, own a pair of jeans?" he asked again.

"Of course."

"Well?"

"Well, what?"

"You can't ride in all that finery." He pointed

to her skirt which contained several yards of undoubtedly expensive silk in mingled shades of turquoise and lavender. Not to mention the matching silk blouse.

"Ride? Horses?"

He needed this kind of grief like he needed a hole in his head, but the lady obviously didn't need to be running around loose. "Horsepower. I'm talking about this motorcycle. You know..." He held out his hands as if gripping imaginary handlebars, twisting them forward. "...varo-o-o-m, varo-o-o-m."

"But I couldn't possibly—"

"It's the only way you're leaving here, unless, of course, you want to walk."

"Aren't you even going to look at the car? Maybe you could fix whatever is wrong with it."

"Don't know anything about cars."

"I thought all guys knew about cars," Paige insisted.

"Not this guy."

"But you don't understand. I desperately need to be in Houston by tonight. Eight a.m. tomorrow at the latest. I've got a job interview at ten o'clock and it's my only chance. The man is leaving on a buying trip tomorrow afternoon."

Dog-tired and his patience wearing thin, Logan was beginning to regret that he'd stopped. He wouldn't leave her, of course, but maybe a little fear might get her off her high horse.

"You know, Rusty, for a desperate woman you sure are picky. This is not Burger King and you don't get everything your way. Personally, I don't give a tinker's damn where you have to be.

All I'm offering is a ride into the next town. From there you can get a plane, train or a hot air balloon for all I care."

"But, I couldn't possibly ride on—"

"Duchess, if you say, 'I couldn't possibly,' one more time, I swear I'm going to turn my back and walk the hell away from you so fast it'll make your head spin."

"But I couldn't—" She stopped short at the warning in his eyes. "I mean…I…I've never ridden on a motorcycle in my life."

"There's only one rule: Don't fall off."

"Look, I appreciate what you did, but—"

"What I did was save your life, which will probably be a short one if you continue with this attitude."

Attitude? He had the nerve to say she had an attitude?

"In fact, at this rate, you're probably going to wind up on a slab with an ID tag dangling from your big toe."

"Y-you don't have to be so…so crude!"

"Hey, if crude is what it takes to get my point across, then crude it is, Duchess."

"Stop calling me that."

Logan shrugged and started walking around to the other side of the motorcycle.

Surely he wouldn't just leave her here. Of course not, she thought, watching him swing his leg over the seat and stick the key in the ignition. He strapped on his helmet. "You're not leaving, are you?"

"What's it look like?"

It looked like he was leaving.

Paige stared at him, desperation warring with caution. "But, I…I…"

"Be happy to stop at the first garage and tell them you need a tow," he said so calmly Paige wanted to slap him.

"You'd just leave me here, stranded? Easy prey for another pair of opportunists?" She was totally out of her element. Her only hope was to bluff her way through this situation. The only problem was that he wasn't going for it. So, it was Logan Walker or… She didn't even want to think about the "or." "All right, I'll go with you."

When she didn't move after a moment or two he removed his helmet and stared at her. For the first time she noticed his eyes were blue, clear as a Rocky Mountain lake, then the next second berated herself for even noticing. What did she care what color his eyes were? Some women probably even thought he was handsome. And to be fair, she had to admit there was a raw sensuality about the man. Hard to detect behind that lazy walk and talk, but it was there in his eyes. Very elemental, very male. Tall, broad-shouldered with some well-defined biceps, he looked like he could handle whatever the world dished out, but the rest of him was well…scruffy, or maybe rough around the edges was a better description. His hair was wavy and a little too long, almost but not quite to the point of being unruly. No doubt, some women found that appealing. As for his clothes, his jeans, T-shirt and jacket were nothing short of ragged. Not the kind of man she was accustomed to, but then this wasn't the kind of situation she was accustomed to, either.

"Thought you were in a hurry," he said, jolting her from her perusal.

"What?"

"You're not getting any closer to Houston standing there, so how about getting into those jeans."

"And just where do you propose I change?"

Those clear blue eyes darkened with impatience. "If there's not enough room in that pricey little coupe of yours—"

"I told you it's not mine."

"Whatever. If there's not room for you to wiggle your fanny into the jeans, then open the door, sit in the seat, stretch your legs out and do the best you can," he said as if he were explaining to a child.

The man was intent on humiliating her and that's all there was to it. Well, she'd show him. "Thank you." Paige smiled and marched across the road. The trunk was still open and she grabbed her suitcase, opened it and rummaged through the contents. "Oh, no."

"I don't like the sound of that, Red."

In her haste to leave Denver she'd just grabbed the suitcase she'd packed for the honeymoon. Since Regi was a petite five-foot-three to her five-foot-nine, borrowing clothes had been impossible. She realized the contents of her bag were very limited. Her first order of business upon arriving in Houston would be to buy some new clothes.

"I...I don't know what I was thinking. I mean, I forgot... I didn't bring any jeans with me."

"Then put on whatever you've got."

Irritated at his callous indifference to her plight, she picked up the entire suitcase, walked around and tossed it onto the front seat. "The least you can do is turn around," she told him over the roof of the car.

Still sitting on the motorcycle, Logan turned his head, wondering just what the hell he'd gotten himself into. Ms. O-O'Neil wasn't being straight with him, beginning with her name. But why? Maybe his assessment of her wasn't as dead-on as he'd thought. And maybe the car had been "borrowed" without permission. Possible, but all his instincts were telling him she wasn't a criminal. She might be running, but he didn't think it was from the law.

Of course, where women were concerned he didn't have the best track record. He'd been fooled before. Lord knows his ex-wife had done a first-rate job. She'd given the appearance of wealth and class, but she'd turned out to be a cheap little liar and a cheat. She knew about money, all right. His. She'd gone to great lengths to win him with promises of undying love when all she really wanted was access to his family's money. He'd been wrong about Cindi, but damned few women had fooled him since.

And he'd made sure he didn't make the same mistake twice.

After a nasty divorce with endless haggling over a settlement, he'd left Sweetwater Springs. He'd kept in touch with his grandmother until she passed away a year ago, but since he was an only child and his mother had died before he even started school, there wasn't much family left. His dad had remarried three years ago and had a new young wife who loved to travel. After his experience with Cindi, Logan had turned his back on family money, specifically, a sizable trust fund. Everything he had, he'd earned himself and he liked it that way. At least now he knew the women he dated were interested in him, plain and poor. So far it had worked for him.

His friend Cade McBride had warned him that he was just fooling himself. That one day Fate would put a honey of a woman smack dab in the middle of his path, and it wouldn't make any difference if she had millions or pennies. He'd be a goner. But then, Cade had been separated from his brand-new wife at the time, so how much did he know? Besides, Logan didn't believe in Fate.

He had no use for women who made money the center of their world, be it someone else's money or their own, and Paige O'Neil had all the earmarks of such a woman. Yet…there was something about her that intrigued him. Despite his instinct that she wasn't a criminal, she was hiding something. Or else why the alias? Why the rush to Houston? Yeah, this redhead was a puzzle, he decided, putting on his helmet. And nothing interested him more than a puzzle.

"I, uh, I'm sorry. Everything I've got is resort wear."

Logan turned back and was grateful the helmet's darkly tinted shield prevented her from seeing the stunned expression on his face or the fact that his mouth literally dropped open. She came toward him in a very chic shorts set and the most spectacular pair of legs God ever created.

Some men liked big breasts. Others favored a nicely rounded fanny. Logan was a leg man. The longer the better. Hers were long, slim perfection. It didn't take much for his imagination to see them encased in black silk stockings or better still, bare and wrapped around his waist. He'd been a private investigator too long to accept much of anything at face value but it was hard to ignore the best-looking pair of legs he'd ever seen. The rest of her wasn't bad either. And every stride of those fantastic legs reminded him it had been a while since he'd been with a woman. Damn, she looked good. So good that straddling a motorcycle was suddenly a very uncomfortable position.

No time for this, he told himself, but only half-heartedly. He'd bet a hundred dollars she wasn't a serial killer, but she was definitely in the running for the sexiest woman he'd seen in a long time.

"That's, uh...that's the best you can do? You telling me you don't have one pair of pants in that suitcase?"

"Yes, but they're made out of very flimsy fabric, almost see-through. The rest is shorts, T-shirts and bathing suits."

"That's what you planned to wear in Houston?"

"No, I..." She glanced away. "These clothes were meant for another trip that didn't happen."

"Where to? A nude beach?"

"That's none of your business." He had no idea how close he'd come to the truth. She and Randal had planned to honeymoon on a private island and nude bathing had definitely been on the agenda.

"Go back and put on the pants, Rusty."

"But they're—"

"Flimsy is better than nothing."

She glared at him for a second then turned and stomped back to the car. In two minutes she was back wearing the pants and a matching sleeveless shirt. The shirttails were tied in a knot just under her breasts, leaving her midriff bare.

He was wrong. Flimsy wasn't better than nothing.

At least with bare legs he knew what he was up against, but this... The breeze turned the thin, airy fabric into a curtain for a peek show. It molded itself to her legs and hips then flowed away only to tease him with a repeat performance. When she said "almost transparent" she wasn't kidding. He could practically see right through to her...

Logan blinked, convinced his imagination was working overtime. It wasn't. God almighty, she was wearing the skimpiest bikini underwear he'd ever seen!

For a second he thought about telling her to change back into the shorts, but decided the hassle wouldn't be worth it. She would just want to know why and he wasn't about to tell her the truth. Namely, that he still didn't want her money, but her body was looking more tempting by the minute.

He'd been celibate too long. That was the problem. Two demanding, time-consuming cases back-to-back had robbed him of any time for socializing with the softer sex. Naturally, any reasonably attractive, well-put-together female would be tempting. Naturally. And if he told himself that long enough he might begin to believe it.

Then she stopped right in front of him and took a deep breath, straining his belief system. The shirt, already pulled tight across her breasts by the knot, got tighter. So did Logan's groin.

She held up her purse. "What do I do with this?"

He was supposed to be telling himself something about any reasonably attractive female, but at the moment he couldn't remember what. Whatever it was, reason had nothing to do with the thoughts and images in his head and everything to do with good old-fashioned, long-denied lust. And as for Ms. O-O'Neil, she was probably trouble on the hoof, but he'd never seen better-looking hooves in his life.

It was only for four miles, Logan reminded himself, carefully sliding off the bike, taking the purse and stuffing it into the saddlebag. He was a mature, intelligent man. He could keep from drooling for four miles. All he had to do was keep his eyes on the road and his thoughts focused on driving.

"C'mon." He handed her his helmet, helped her on with it then showed her how to step up and onto the Harley. "The sooner we get to Texline, the better."

2

THEY WERE THE longest four miles Logan had ever driven, and he actually breathed a sigh of relief when they passed the Texline city-limits sign. He whipped into the driveway of the first decent-sized garage.

"Thanks," Paige said, as soon as he killed the engine and she could be heard.

He got off, reached to help her but she had already swung those long, luscious legs over the seat and was standing. "Sure." He couldn't get her off his bike and out of his life fast enough. Keeping his eyes on the road had been easy. Keeping his thoughts off that glimpse of her bikini underwear was a different story. It was a good thing their paths were about to split. After all, a man could only stand so much temptation.

As she removed the helmet then handed it to him, she gave her head a shake and it tumbled about her shoulders like red-gold flames dancing in the breeze. When she brushed it back from her face the diamonds in her ears caught the glint of the sun.

"And thanks again for coming to my rescue. Not every man would have been so fearless." As soon as she spoke, Paige realized how truly fearless he'd been.

Logan Walker had risked his life to rescue her.

When he stopped, he had no idea if the men were friendly. For all he knew they could have had guns, too. In fact, they might have killed him. She had seen firsthand that his ex-cop sensibilities were still highly functional, so he had to have been aware of the possible danger. But he still stopped. He still faced down two strangers in a situation that could have gotten ugly. If that wasn't the definition of a hero, she didn't know what was. Suddenly her desire for freedom and independence carried a high price tag in light of what it might have cost Logan.

He pulled her purse from the saddlebag and practically shoved it at her. "Don't go pinning any medals on me."

Okay, so he was an insolent hero. "Well, you deserve one. And I mean that. You did something I believe very few people would have done. It was my good fortune that you came along. Thank you." She held out her hand.

Logan took her hand, intending a quick, impersonal shake, but it didn't turn out that way. The minute he touched her the jolt of raw sexual heat hit him like a sucker punch to the jaw. For a second he thought he actually saw stars.

"No big deal." He released her hand. "Uh, good luck with your car."

Paige turned and walked toward the garage bay entrance hoping he didn't notice that her steps were slightly unsteady. The same could be said for her heartbeat. What was that…strange little zing and lingering heat she noticed the minute he touched her? A sort of tingling sensation as if she had accidentally hit her funny bone and burned herself at the same time. Except it wasn't funny. It was…exciting.

Logan watched her, his senses spinning like a rank bull straight out of the chute. He'd never experienced anything like what had just happened. And he was no inexperienced kid when it came to women. Years spent in calf-roping competition on the rodeo circuit gave him enough exposure to eager buckle bunnies to know instant lust when he saw it. Or felt it. And there was definitely lust involved a minute ago, but there was something else—something hot and deep sparking a hunger he hadn't felt in a long time.

Yeah, he wanted to yank her into his arms for a deep taste of her mouth. And he wanted her melting over him like homemade ice cream at a Fourth of July picnic. Hell, he wanted to throw her back on the bike, find the nearest motel and make love to her until they were both breathless and senseless. And then…

Then he wanted to hold her. Just hold her, feel her soft sexy body next to his all night and make love to her again at sunrise. Logan shook his head. Strange thoughts. The lust he could handle. The longing he wasn't so sure about.

"You're losing it, Walker," he mumbled.

He'd known the woman all of two hours and he was fantasizing about her. Fatigue, pure and simple. Too much work. He'd be fine once he was in Sweetwater Springs. Nothing like a hometown and friends that knew all his faults and liked him anyway. He'd done his good deed for the day. She was safe and sound and he could be on his way.

Intending a casual wave goodbye, Logan glanced up to see Paige O'Neil frantically rummaging through her purse. A mechanic in greasy overalls stood by looking bored.

"Aw, hell." Practically before he finished his comment, Paige ran back to him.

"It's gone! My money, credit cards. All…gone!"

"Figures." If he'd been thinking with anything above his waist he'd have told her to check her purse and suitcase before they drove away. "Were either of those jerks that stopped to help you inside your car at any time?"

"No. Yes. The stocky one. He flipped the lever to open the hood and the trunk but he was sitting on the passenger side."

"And your purse was on the seat, right?"

Realization dawned. "Oh, no. I…I was talking to the other man, and not paying any attention…"

"That's how they work. Got a feeling those guys were old pros. If it makes you feel any better, you probably weren't the only one they hit today."

"It doesn't," she whispered, clutching her purse to her like a shield.

He was going to kill Rick when he got back to Denver, because right now it was easier to blame his partner's prophetic words than admit to their truth. Puzzles and cries for help. Paige O'Neil certainly fit both criteria. She hadn't actually asked for help but the request was there in her eyes. She had that little lost puppy look, and as much as he wanted to ignore it, Logan knew he wouldn't. Damn Rick, anyway.

"All right. Climb on," he told her. "We'll go on over to the police station and you can file charges. Between the two of us we should be able to give them a damn good description and—"

"I—I'm… No thanks."

"Whatdaya mean, 'no thanks'? You need to file charges on those creeps. The paperwork is gonna take at least an hour and that'll put me in Sweetwater Springs near midnight. So, the sooner we get to it, the sooner we'll finish. Now c'mon. Don't give me a hard time about this."

She looked at Logan, her eyes swimming with restrained tears. She couldn't tell him the real reason she couldn't go to the cops. What was she going to do, give them a phony name? How smart would that be? If she gave them her real name it might become another clue for whatever detective was on her trail. But her excuse would have to be logical or she was certain Logan would question it.

"I'm not trying to give you a hard time, but what's the use? I'm not a citizen in this community or even this state. How much time do you think the local officers are going to spend on such a case? And even if they caught the guys, and the chance of that is remote, the money would be gone. A phone call cancels the credit cards. Except for the fact that I'm a much poorer, but wiser person, what's the point?"

As much as Logan hated to admit it, she was

right. Even the police would agree. Her chances of recovering the money were slim to none, and Slim left town.

"They get your checkbook?"

"What?"

"If they got your checkbook you need to call your bank so they can stop payment on any checks those sleazoids may try to pass. When you explain what happened, I'm sure the bank will work with you to set up a new account. Whatever it takes so you can get to your—"

"I don't have a bank account," she lied. "I closed it because I was moving to Houston."

"Traveler's checks?" She shook her head. "You mean to tell me you were driving around with a wad of cash in your purse?"

"Not very much. That's why I need this job."

"A job you're not even sure you've got."

"I—I made up my mind to start a new life. New city. New job. I closed all my accounts, said goodbye to everything. Out with the old, in with the new. Is that so hard to understand?"

Logan shrugged. "So…what now? Call your folks?"

"No! Out of the question."

That sounded like not only no, but hell no, Logan thought. So she wasn't close to her family. He knew from personal experience how easily it could happen. "Got someone else you can call? How about the rich friend who loaned you the car?"

"She flew to New York this morning to catch the Concorde to Paris."

"No other friends or relatives?"

Nervously, she twisted the strap of her purse. "No, but I'll be fine. In two, maybe three hours I'll be able to reach my friend when she checks into her Paris hotel."

"Red, in two or three hours you're gonna be the only person awake in this burg. They roll up the sidewalks when the sun goes down, and—" he shaded his eyes, gauging the angle of the sun on the horizon "—that's gonna happen in about another hour."

"I'll be fine," she lied, knots of dread already forming in the pit of her stomach. "My friend will wire me some money then I can get a room—"

"Wire you some money? I doubt Texline has a Western Union office and if they do, it closes early. Take a look around. This isn't exactly a metropolitan area. You've got a couple of gas stations, this garage, a café, a two-bit motel and the obligatory First Baptist Church. Sugar, in case you haven't realized it, this town is just a wide spot in the road."

"I know that." Did he take her for a complete idiot? "And I realize the car will have to be towed to the next largest city with a Jaguar dealership—"

"Which is probably Amarillo. That's over ninety miles away."

"Ninety miles!"

"Yeah." What had started out as a good deed was turning into a bad deal for both of them. He was losing time and she was...well, she was losing all the way around. "And my guess is Mack the Mechanic over there isn't going to be in a big hurry without having some big bucks waved at him. Which we've already established you don't have. Of course, you could leave the car as collateral."

Paige took a deep breath. "No. I'd rather not."

Okay, so there were a few obstacles. Her road to self-reliance had developed a few unexpected hairpin curves, and she might have to postpone her life, liberty and pursuit of happiness for a while. He didn't have to keep waving it in front of her like a red cape at a bull, did he? She would just have to come up with an alternative plan. Fast.

One thing she wasn't going to do was cry on Logan Walker's shoulder. He'd made it clear this was the end of the road as far as he was concerned. If he expected her to fall apart and beg him not to leave, he was sadly mistaken.

"So, what are you gonna do?"

"Well…"

"Actually, you've just about run out of options."

Her nerves were already frayed and his casual assessment of her situation was irritating in the extreme. She wasn't sure if she was angrier at herself for the carelessness that got her into this mess in the first place, or him for reminding her of it. Dammit, she was doing the best she could. "Did anyone ever tell you that you're pushy?"

"A time or two."

She wanted him to go away and take this unpleasant situation with him, but at the same time she didn't want to be left alone. How's that for a dichotomy? Unreasonable, she knew. While her mind knew fear bred her unreasonability, emotionally she really wished she could blame Logan for everything. She was mad at him, madder at herself.

"You know, just because you…you—"

"Saved your life."

"Just because you helped me out of a bad situation doesn't mean I now belong to you. This isn't China. You're free to be on your merry way." She gave a wave of dismissal. "I absolve you of all responsibility."

Well, if that didn't take the cake. Here he was trying to bail her saucy little butt out of a jam and she gets snippy. "You know damned good and well I'm going to drive away and leave you standing here."

"Why not? You were certainly willing to leave me on the side of the road."

"That was before I knew you were broke and alone," he snapped. "My grandmother raised me better than to turn away from anybody who's down and out."

Her hands curled into fists. That was the final insult. The final arrow piercing her already wounded pride. "I am not…"

Paige cut herself off, stunned at how close she'd come to telling him she wasn't broke, that she had more money than he could imagine. The look of pity in his eyes had almost pushed her to say too much. Her pride nicked, she'd nearly blurted out, *I have money. I just can't get to it at the moment.*

And she could imagine his response. With his ego he'd probably think she was making it up.

Easy, she told herself, and with the first deep breath came an idea. A sort of reverse psychology strategy. It was a feeble attempt, but she was afraid that as long as he thought she was "down and out" he would insist on helping, even if that meant calling in some sort of agency or, God forbid, the police.

So, if she'd told him the truth and he thought she was lying, then if she lied would he believe her?

"I'm not broke," she announced.

"You're not?"

"My mad money."

"What?"

"In all of the turmoil I forgot about my mad money," she lied. "I always keep a hundred-dollar bill tucked into a hiding place in my makeup case."

"Uh-huh."

She smiled. "I can't believe it completely slipped my mind. What a relief. Now I can pay for the tow and get a room. I'll call my friend in Paris, and I'm sure she's got some kind of insurance to take care of things like this."

"And just how are you going to get to your makeup case?"

"Oh." She twisted the purse strap harder. "Well, uh, it'll be in the car when they tow it in, right?"

"Uh-huh."

"Then I'll have money. Problem solved. Everything is fine."

Oh, yeah. Everything was just dandy except she was lying through those luscious lips of hers.

If she'd told him to butt out, or even to drop dead, he'd have been fine with that. But her valiant—pitiful, but valiant—attempt to lie got him right in the heart. "Aw, hell," he whispered.

"I beg your pardon?"

"Do yourself a favor, Rusty. Don't ever try to earn a living playing poker."

"I don't—"

"You're a rotten liar."

"And you are the rudest man I've ever met," she said with what she hoped was just the right touch of indignation.

"No, I'm just a man who wants to get home for a little peace and quiet. And that includes not waking up in the middle of the night wondering if you're lying in a ditch somewhere."

Logan got off the bike, hung his helmet on one of the handlebars, then walked to the back and unlocked the "trunk" mounted behind the seat. He took out his wallet then looked at Paige. "I respect pride. Got enough of it myself to know it can hamper as well as help, but I do respect it. And trust me when I say you can't eat it, or sleep on it. So, what's it gonna be?" He held up the wallet. "A loan, or your pride?"

"Really, I don't need—"

"There's no mad money, is there?"

"I don't know what you mean." The bluff didn't sound substantial even to her own ears.

Logan shook his head. She had tenacity, he'd give her that much. "What if I'd believed you?"

He was right, she was a rotten liar. Even as a child she hadn't been able to tell a decent lie. Okay, so she was caught. Now she had to face the music with as much dignity as possible. Paige looked up, then away, praying her voice wouldn't shake. "I—I don't know."

"All right. I'll loan you enough money—"

"But, I couldn't possibly—"

"Duchess, you need to scratch the phrase, 'couldn't possibly' from your vocabulary. Now, didn't you say you had a friend who would send you some money?"

"Yes, but—"

"Well then, this is how I see it. I can cover the towing, give you a little extra for a room, then you can just mail me a check when you get your money."

"You mean...I'd stay here?"

He nodded. "Or, I cover the towing and we ride on. The second option works better from where I stand. I get home, and by the time we get to Lubbock you'll be able to reach your friend, plus you'll be two hundred and fifty miles closer to Houston. You can get yourself a good night's sleep then catch an early morning flight out and probably still make your interview. This way we both get what we want."

It was one thing to accept a short ride in broad daylight out of desperation. It was another to accept money, ride several more hours and end up at his home. At night. For the first time since Logan had rescued her, Paige wondered if he had ulterior motives. She might not be the most experienced woman on the block, but she knew lust when she saw it. And she'd seen the way he looked at her legs. What if—

Logan started to laugh.

"What's so…funny?" she asked.

"You should see your face right now. I can read it like a newspaper. All of a sudden it's dawned on you that I might be making plans to get you out in the middle of nowhere and," he twirled an imaginary mustache, "have my way with you."

Her cheeks warmed with embarrassment. "Well…"

"If that's what I'd wanted, I could've jumped you while you were changing, hauled you off into the tall grass beside the road and done whatever I wanted to you. Nobody would have seen us. But that's not my style. I've never forced a woman in my life." His voice dropped to an intimate tone. "Never had to. Any time a woman wants me, all she has to do is say so."

And she didn't doubt plenty had done just that. "I—I see your point."

"Besides, you took a leap of faith back on that highway," he pointed out. "This is just another step."

He made it all sound so easy. "You know this is crazy, don't you? Until a couple of hours ago we'd never laid eyes on each other. Now here you are offering to trust me with your hard-earned money and I'm trusting you not to…"

"Take advantage of the situation?"

"Yes. And speaking of taking advantage, what makes you think I won't hop a plane and forget I ever saw you or your money?"

"Instincts. Mine are telling me you're on the up-and-up."

He'd be surprised how far off his instincts

were, she thought. Maybe she should take a chance and tell him who she was. What if one of her mother's paid bloodhounds had already picked up the scent and eventually found out Logan had helped her? She didn't want any trouble directed at him because of her. But she didn't want any trouble for herself either. And she had to admit it certainly sounded like the best solution.

"What about your family? What will they think when you show up with a strange woman in tow?"

"No problem. I'll find you a room in Lubbock, then head home—"

"Isn't that where you live?"

"Nope. A little town about ten miles southwest of Lubbock called Sweetwater Springs."

His plan was simple and direct. With it, he'd effectively removed all the obstacles, straightened all the hairpin curves on this particular stretch of her road to self-reliance. If she stayed in Texline, she would have to rent a car or take a bus to Amarillo, the nearest decent-size airport. And she doubted she could do either tonight, much less book a flight to Houston. Her chances of making the interview in time nosedived. On the other hand, she could be in Lubbock by midnight and fly out early tomorrow morning. She would be cutting the time close, but her chances were at least fifty percent better.

As unusual as this situation was, Paige realized, if nothing else, the events of the day had proven that she could think on her feet and that hopeless was only a word, not a sentence for fail-

ure. And as for Logan, well… He might not look
like a knight in shining armor or have the manners of a southern gentleman, but there was
something solid and honest about him. Even
though the thought had crossed her mind to
question his motives, she'd never actually felt
threatened by him. She trusted him.

Maybe she had listened to her instincts without realizing it, just as he had. If so, he was right.
She *had* made a leap of faith the minute she
agreed to let him help her. "All right," she said.
"I'll ride with you."

He grinned, then patted his stomach. "I'm so
hungry my belly is rubbin' against my backbone.
How 'bout you?"

Paige blinked at the unexpected question. "As
a matter of fact, I am hungry."

He handed her twenty dollars and his calling
card. "While I go back for your clothes, why
don't you call the credit card companies, then after you're finished, go across the street to that
café and grab us a couple of burgers."

"Okay."

He swung his right leg over the seat and
started the engine. "Make mine the biggest one
they've got, a large order of fries and a chocolate
malt. Oh yeah," he added as he put on his helmet, "I like lots of onions." With a twist of the
handlebars, the engine revved and he was gone.

Paige watched him go, then glanced at the
money in her hand. Had she made the right decision? Staying in Texline was not going to get
her where she wanted to be. Going with Logan
would. It was just that simple. Of course, if she

were being honest, she had to admit that the unhappy prospect of being left alone might have
swayed her decision—

No. She wasn't going to start second-guessing
herself.

She might not have been responsible for her
original dilemma, but truthfully she hadn't
helped matters when she went running off without a backup or contingency plan. The milk was
spilled and tears wouldn't help. Now, she had to
get herself out of this mess the best way she
could.

And for the moment, Logan Walker was the
best way.

TWENTY MINUTES LATER, with Paige's suitcase
strapped on the back of the bike, Logan was riding back to Texline, haunted by his own words to
Rick.

It's your job to save the world for the next month.

Obviously, he hadn't abided by his own edict.
Not only had he rescued Paige O'Neil, now he
was hauling her all the way to Lubbock and
loaning her money to boot. He told himself it
was because she needed his help and there was
no one else. That this really was the most logical
solution to the problem. But while his mind was
telling him he'd handled the whole thing simply
and logically, his body was sending him a different message altogether. Like, those long legs of
hers had no effect on his decision whatsoever.
Yeah, right. And that tantalizing glimpse of bikini underwear wasn't a factor either. Uh-huh.

Okay, okay, so she turned him on. He'd have

to be dead for her not to. But the truth was Paige O'Neil interested him in more ways than one.

He was definitely convinced she was running from something. Or somebody. His money was on somebody. She'd gone white as a ghost when he'd mentioned he used to be a cop. He could imagine her reaction if she knew he was a private investigator. Maybe he'd just keep that to himself for a while.

A while?

What was he thinking? Four more hours and she would be out of his life. He doubted the subject of what he did for a living would even come up. No reason for it to. After all, they'd probably never see each other again after tonight, and that was fine with him. No matter how good-looking she was, he still had a feeling Paige was trouble. So why in the world had he stopped in the first place? Maybe Rick was right.

Maybe he was a sucker for trouble.

3

"WE'VE GOT ONE more item to take care of before we head out," Logan told Paige as he polished off the last of his French fries and malt. "You still can't ride in those clothes."

"But—"

"It's almost dark." He nodded toward the front window of the restaurant. "When the sun goes down, so does the temperature."

"It was nearly eighty today. How far can it drop?"

"Even if the thermometer says it's eighty degrees, the air moving over your body as you ride will be a lot cooler, especially at night and on practically bare legs."

She found that hard to believe. A little devil sitting on her shoulder wondered if he wasn't exaggerating just to exercise the control he seemed to enjoy. "But you know this is all I have."

Logan slid out of the booth they were sharing, stood up, then picked up a small empty canvas bag he'd brought in with him. "I think I've got it covered. While I settle the bill and wash up, why don't you go out to the bike and decide which of those clothes you absolutely have to have. Put whatever you're taking in here." He handed her the bag.

"Why?"

"Because, Ms. Clotheshorse, there's not enough room to take all of your clothes. Here." He gave her his keys. "Open the back trunk. You'll have to make room for your bag. And make it snappy. We need to get on the road."

"And what do I do with my suitcase?"

Logan sighed. "Sell it, or give it away. I don't care."

Paige scooted out of the booth and grabbed her purse. "I thought an empty stomach might be partly responsible for your grumpiness. Looks like I was wrong." And she walked out.

Ten minutes later Logan found her peering into the trunk, shuffling his things around. "Did you find enough— Where's the cooler?"

Paige looked up. "The what?"

"The cooler. The softside cooler. About the size of a kid's lunch box."

"Oh, it's over there."

Logan glanced toward a patch of grass near the front of the bike. There, indeed, was the cooler. Open and empty. "Where's my beer?"

"I poured it out."

"You what!"

Paige jumped. "Don't yell like that. You scared me."

"You better be lying or I'll do more than scare you. So help me I'll wring your—"

"You told me to make room for my bag in the trunk."

"I didn't tell you to pitch my beer!"

"What was I supposed to get rid of?" she yelled back. "Call me crazy, but I didn't think you'd want me to get rid of your tools. You know, just in case you might need them to repair this silly machine. So, that left a baseball cap, a plastic pouch, another helmet and the cooler. The pouch contained what looked like registration and insurance information. I assumed the helmet was necessary and expensive so it stayed. The baseball cap—"

"You didn't. Tell me you didn't—"

"—was autographed by Nolan Ryan. Now, I may not know anything about cars, but I know men and sports. I *knew* it stayed. That left the cooler." She took a deep breath, running out of steam and air at the same time, and put her hands on her hips. "So, sue me."

Logan stared at her, trying hard to control his temper. If he didn't, he was afraid he would kill her. "Did it ever cross your mind," he said as calmly as he could, "to wait and ask me?"

Paige glared at him. "You told me to make it snappy!"

He started to say something then decided he would probably say too much. And even though he hated to admit it, fair was fair. He *had* told her to hurry and he hadn't put any restrictions on what she had to do to make room for her things. Next time, and God forbid there was one, he'd explain himself better. "Just...get your clothes in the bag and let's get the hell out of here."

"Fine by me." Paige stepped up to the open suitcase and grabbed a handful of lacy bras and panties. "How much can I take?"

"If it doesn't fit in that bag, it doesn't go."

"You've got to be—" Logan cut her a warning

look. "Never mind. I'll get whatever I need in Houston."

"Oh, I've no doubt. Shop till you drop."

"Do you have something against money?" Paige asked at the unmistakable bitterness in his voice.

"Nope."

"So, then it's just women with money?"

"With it, looking for it."

"A woman must have wreaked some serious financial havoc in your life." The look in his eyes told her she had stepped on an emotional land mine.

"The word gold digger was invented for my ex-wife."

"Obviously, the experience left you jaded, but—"

"Jaded? Try smarter. Next time I'll recognize a liar and a cheat from a long way off."

"What on earth did she do to you?" The question popped out before she could stop it. "I'm sorry. That's none of my business."

He shrugged. "No big deal. I had more than a few coins in my pocket and knew to be cautious. But she was clever, pretending to come from money so it looked like she was only interested in me. Once she had me hooked, it didn't take long for her to show her true colors. All she cared about was getting her hands on everything I owned."

"We're not all greedy little schemers, you know," she told him, truly sorry he'd had a lousy experience, and no matter what he said, she suspected it was a big deal. She went back to rummaging through her things, stuffing some into the bag, discarding others. "Some of us might have gotten used to the finer things in life, but that doesn't mean we can't live without them."

She had no sooner got the words out of her mouth than she pulled out the exquisite and outrageously expensive ivory negligee she had intended to wear on her wedding night. Good riddance, she thought, glad to leave behind any reminders of Randal the Rat and everything he represented.

Logan took one look at the nearly transparent gown and a mental image of her wearing it streaked across his mind. "No room for that," he said. Reaching into the saddlebag compartment on his side of the motorcycle he pulled out a pair of his jeans and a belt. "Go inside and put these on."

Paige took the jeans and tossed the negligee at him. It hit him square in the chest, the gossamer fabric cascading down his arm. "What the hell am I supposed to do with this?" he called as she walked away from him.

"Sell it, or give it away. I don't care."

Logan crushed the delicate fabric in his hand as another erotic image flashed across his mind. "Aw, hell," he muttered. He tossed the gown into the suitcase, snapped it shut, then carried it across the parking lot and flung it into the dumpster.

It took Paige only five minutes to change, due to the way the jeans fit. Or didn't fit was more accurate. In fact, they were so roomy she had to use both hands to hold them up as she walked. "They won't stay up," she explained as she approached the bike with double handfuls of denim and the belt dangling from a belt loop.

Logan shook his head. "That's what the belt is for."

"It's too big, too."

"Aw, hell."

Before Paige realized his intentions, he grabbed the waistband of the jeans and yanked her to him. She lost her balance and fell forward. The next thing she knew his arm was around her waist and they were so close they practically bumped chins.

"Oh, I—" Struggling to right herself, she clutched at his jacket, missed and ended up with a fistful of his T-shirt. Then she lifted her gaze to his and forgot about falling, about everything but looking into his eyes. She'd been wrong to compare them to anything as simple as clear blue, or as calm as a mountain lake. Up close—and she was very close—the irises were ringed in a blue as dark as the deepest ocean and flecked with white. His eyes were incredibly intense. Hot. The kind of heat only passion generates. That instinctive animal sexuality that set a man apart from other men and made women want to be as close to him as possible. It wasn't hard for her to understand how a woman could surrender to that kind of heat and power. Not hard at all.

Paige might have been the one to lose her footing, but Logan wasn't too steady himself at the moment. He couldn't stop staring at her lips, soft, pink and slightly parted. Inviting. So inviting he had a hard time dealing with the sudden burst of heat spiraling through his body. She was a sweet armful and he wanted a taste. Wanted to run his tongue along those soft lips, accept their honeyed invitation and... Digging deep, he found just enough willpower to do the right thing. He set her back on her feet. "I didn't, uh, mean to pull so hard."

"No, it's... I just wasn't expecting..." He glanced down at her hand still clutching his shirt. "Sorry," she said, and tried to smooth the wrinkled cotton.

"Don't worry about it," he insisted, wanting her to stop, and regretting it when she did. Logan cleared his throat. "We need to fix these jeans." Moving quickly, he worked the belt through the loops and cinched the buckle into the last hole. When he finished it was obvious this wasn't going to work. The jeans hung on her hips so precariously it looked as if a deep breath would be all it would take to send the jeans to her ankles.

"You see the problem," she said.

"I see it." He studied the sagging jeans for a second, then turned around and reached into his saddlebag again. This time he pulled out a bandanna and tossed it onto the seat of the Harley. Then he unbuckled the belt and started to pull it from the loops. To make sure he didn't accidentally jerk her into his arms again, Logan put a hand on her waist to steady her.

Too bad it didn't have the same effect on him. Who would have thought that little curve of a

woman's waist could be so tantalizing, so erotic?
Who would have thought that much heat could
be concentrated in such a small spot?

"Now what?"

"What?"

"You've removed the belt, now how do I keep
these jeans up?"

He picked up the bandanna, folded it diago-
nally, then rolled it into a makeshift rope. He
handed it to her, stepped away and stuck his
hands into his back pockets. "Just thread it
through the loops then tie it," he instructed, deciding it was better she did it herself. He didn't
want to touch her again. No, he did. And that
was the problem. This wasn't some cold beer
and hot-sex buckle bunny interested in a one-
night stand. This was a love me or leave me,
high-maintenance kind of woman. Not his type.

When Paige finished, the jeans were secure.
Baggy, but secure. "Resourceful," she commented, gazing at the results. "Thanks." But
when she looked up he didn't seem pleased at
all. He was frowning.

"You can thank me by getting your keister on
the bike so we can get the hell out of here." He
turned and crammed her bag into the trunk.

"You wouldn't by any chance have another
bandanna, would you?"

Logan slammed the trunk shut. "What for?"

"I, uh…" The way he was acting she was almost afraid to tell him. "I—my hair. It whipped
around my face and neck as we rode and I
thought maybe I could tie it back—"

"Sorry. Fresh out," he snapped, handed her

the helmet and helped her onto the bike. End of conversation.

All right, she thought, fastening the chin strap. Maybe he was holding a grudge over the beer thing. But she honestly didn't know what else she could have done. Okay, maybe she should have extended him the courtesy of asking, but how was she to know what he considered indispensable? A few more hours and they would be out of each other's hair, out of each other's lives. Fine. Peachy, in fact. Not that she wasn't grateful for all he'd done. She was. In fact, for a moment or two, something had passed between them, some…connection, for lack of a better word, and she'd thought they might even pass the next few hours at least being polite to each other. Obviously, she was wrong.

Without another word, they rolled out of the restaurant parking lot onto the highway and drove into the night.

THE SHORT TRIP into Texline hadn't prepared Paige for a real ride. She'd seen enough movies to know heroes on motorcycles were too tempting for the heroines to resist, and now she understood why. It wasn't rebellion, although that certainly added spice. It wasn't just a chrome-and-leather jacket mystique. It was power. Wild, fast, seductive power.

The Harley raced over the highway like a panther on the hunt, growling its way through the night. And Paige loved it. She felt the pulsing power of the bike's engine vibrate through her body. Exhilarating. The taste of freedom she'd experienced breezing along in the little green sports car couldn't begin to hold a candle to this feeling of total liberation. This sheer, unfettered abandon. She lost herself in the delicious sensation. So much so, in fact, that time seemed unimportant.

But, gradually, reality intruded on her joy and she realized, once again, Logan had been right. Even though the thermometer registered a pleasant seventy-five degrees, the constant stream of air rushing over her body felt more like forty. With only a T-shirt between her and the night air, soon Paige began to shiver. She hugged her arms to her, leaning as close as she dared to Logan so that his body acted as a shield against the wind. It was little comfort, but she'd be damned if she would complain. No way was she going to be responsible for him losing even one more minute of time. She swore she'd freeze to death before she asked him to stop. When he finally did stop, she would have kissed his feet in gratitude if she hadn't been stiff with cold.

Logan whipped the bike into a filling station/convenience store on the southern outskirts of Amarillo. He hated stopping even for gas, but it was necessary. Besides, fatigue was hammering at him like a blacksmith on an anvil. A shot of caffeine might help. For Paige, too, he thought. She'd been quiet ever since they rode through Dalhart almost an hour and a half ago and he wondered if she had dozed off. If she had, she'd maintained her balance like a veteran rider. He stepped off the bike, unscrewed the lid to the gas tank and reached for the nozzle at the same time.

And realized Paige hadn't made a move to get off the bike. She sat dead still.

"Rusty?" She nodded. "How about some coffee?" She nodded adamantly, but still didn't move. "Hey." He put a hand on her arm and his eyes widened. "God almighty, your skin is as cold as ice." He immediately forgot about pumping gas, unhooked the chin strap and removed her helmet, then started rubbing her arms. As soon as he touched her she started to shiver.

"Why the hell didn't you tell me you were so cold?" She looked at him, shook her head, but said nothing. "Answer me, dammit!"

"D-didn't want-t you to—to lose t-time."

Logan stared at her in disbelief. She was pale as a ghost and so cold her teeth were actually chattering, but she'd toughed it out rather than asked him to stop. "Fool," he whispered, not sure which one of them deserved the title more. He took off his jacket and put it around her shoulders.

Lingering warmth from his body enveloped her and Paige sighed in pure ecstasy.

Talk about feeling like pond scum. If he'd had a ladder he could have gone eye to eye with a snake. He'd been so unnerved by his damned out-of-control hormones while trying to get her into the jeans, he'd deliberately focused all his thoughts on riding and nothing else. Unnerved, then mad. The truth was he'd been mad as hell at himself for being attracted to Paige when he knew nothing could, or would, come of it. And he'd taken his anger out on her. He was a jerk. Okay, a world-class jerk. The least he could do was try and make it up to her during what was left of their time together. He could control his baser instincts for that long.

"C'mon." He helped her off the bike. "Go inside and get us a couple of cups of coffee. I'll be there in a minute."

When he walked into the convenience store to pay for the gas a few moments later, Paige barely glanced up from her cup. She was obviously savoring not only the hot brew but the steam rising from the coffee as well. "I got us both a large. Hope that's okay."

"Fine." He paid then walked over to where she stood by the coffee bar. "Warmer, Red?"

"Yes. Thank you." She started to shrug out of his jacket, but he stopped her.

"Keep it on."

"But—"

"I'm so used to riding in all kinds of temperatures that I didn't stop to think you might be cold. We've got almost two more hours before we reach Lubbock." He took her cup, set it aside, then held his coat so she could slip her arms into the sleeves. Then he zipped the jacket. "If you'll leave this up," he said, turning up the collar, "and put the helmet on over it, it'll keep the wind from whistling down your neck."

"Thanks," she said.

His hands, still holding the collar, framed her face. A face now almost devoid of cosmetics, her cheeks rosy from the wind...and every bit as flawless as the first time he'd seen her. Was that only this afternoon? It felt as if they'd been together for days instead of hours. He'd always avoided the kind of woman that had to have her makeup perfect and not a hair out of place. The kind of woman that wouldn't be caught dead on a Harley. Exactly the kind of woman he assumed Paige to be, yet here she was hanging tough and looking good doing it. Looking downright delicious doing it.

Logan moved his hands away. Those baser instincts again. His tired brain was unleashing some dangerous thoughts. In a couple of hours she would go back to her rich friends, back to her life, leaving him with his. Such as it was. "Drink up," he said. "You can have another if you want."

"No, this is fine. But I do need to," she said, glancing toward the rest room sign, "you know."

"Sure, go ahead."

When Paige walked out of the convenience store, Logan was waiting by the bike and she quickened her steps. "I'm sorry, I didn't realize you were—"

"Here, these should help." He held up what looked like a pair of leather pants with the seat missing. "These are stovepipe chaps. They're too big, but they'll act as a windbreaker."

"Thanks. How do I—"

"Pull them on over your pants. They buckle at the waist."

With one hand on the bike to balance herself, Paige stepped into the chaps. They were indeed too big, but she didn't care. They were warm.

Logan helped her onto the bike, then adjusted her helmet over the jacket's collar just as he'd described. When she was situated, waiting for him to throw his leg over the seat and start the engine, he picked up something from the ground and handed it to her.

A travel mug, with a tight-fitting lid, filled with hot coffee. And a straw so she didn't have to raise the shield of her helmet.

"That should keep you warm for a while." Then without another word or waiting for a thank-you, he started the engine and they were on the road again.

BY THE TIME they took the loop around Lubbock and were nearing the road to Sweetwater Springs, Paige had decided that if the dusty Texas Panhandle didn't make her appreciate the lush green mountains of Colorado nothing ever would. Even under the softness of a full moon, she had never seen a landscape so flat and barren. How, she wondered, had early pioneers, mostly farmers, gazed upon all this vastness and dreamed of making a living from the land? She had once heard this part of Texas described as only good for raising cattle and kids and now she understood why.

She thought about Logan growing up in this area and wondered what his childhood had been like. Had he lived on a ranch or in town? She couldn't quite picture him on horseback with a rope in his hands, but admittedly that was a stereotypical image of ranchers. Maybe he didn't come from a family of ranchers at all. They could be merchants or… It dawned on Paige that basically she knew nothing about Logan except that he lived in a small town, rode a motorcycle and used to be a cop.

Now, there was a piece of information she had conveniently pushed to the back of her mind. But why? It couldn't be because he was so charming he'd made her forget, could it? Or so handsome and sexy that just looking at him made her want to throw herself in his arms and beg him to make love to her.

Where had that thought come from?

Maybe it was because he'd given her the mug of coffee. That gesture, so unexpected, but so appreciated, had touched her deeply. Or maybe it was because their time together was at an end and she could afford to be generous. Whatever the reason, she had to admit that Logan was good-looking. And yes, sexy. She even had to admit that under different circumstances... Afford to be generous? Different circumstances? There she went again, sounding just like a stuffy, let's-keep-everything-under-control Davenport. She *might* be attracted to him? Yes, she was attracted to him. From his appearance to his attitude, he was different from any man she'd ever known.

When she first saw him she thought his hair was too long and he looked rough around the edges. Scruffy was the word she'd used to describe him. Now, she decided the longish hair suited him. He was rough around the edges, but that too, suited his personality. And as for scruffy, she now redefined it as Logan's style. His statement to the world. Straight out it said, "My way." That was it. From the motorcycle to the who-cares wardrobe to the daring rescue, Logan Walker did things his way.

And it made him just about the sexiest, most attractive man she'd ever met.

She ached to sketch him. That jaw and those eyes were better than any life model she'd ever used. She visualized a charcoal sketch. Yes, black and white would do justice to the power and strength in his face, his body. Maybe one of him alone. Another of him on the bike, or maybe…

A nudge from Logan brought her out of her thoughts. He pointed to a sign indicating there was a budget motel at the next exit off the interstate, and she understood he was asking if it was acceptable. Paige nodded, and a few moments later they rolled to a stop in front of the motel office.

Logan dismounted and removed his helmet. "You sure this is okay?"

"I'm sure it'll be fine." She, too, removed her helmet, then hung it on the handlebar as she'd seen him do.

From his wallet he pulled out a calling card and handed it to her. "After you've talked to your friend in Paris, we'll get you a room."

Paige stood there for a moment almost hesitant to go inside. Finally, she smiled. "Bet you were beginning to wonder if you'd ever get rid of a pain in the butt like me."

"I've seen worse." Now that she was about to walk out of his life he discovered he wasn't in that big of a hurry to see her go.

"Logan, I want to thank you for helping me."

She looked into his eyes. "You saved my life and I'll never forget it."

He shrugged. "I told you. It's no big—"

She stepped closer, putting a hand on his arm. "Just accept my thanks. Please."

Logan looked down at her hand and felt the same heat sizzle through his blood as when she'd touched him before. Then he looked at her upturned face, her soft lips parted, and knew he had to taste her just once. Acting on instinct, he slid his hand to the back of her neck as his other arm went around her waist and drew her to him. His mouth took hers in a hungry kiss, seducing and ravishing at the same time.

Paige's initial shock almost instantly gave way to pleasure mixed with a burning need. She put her arm around his neck and hung on, grateful he was holding her because the ground seemed to have vanished from beneath her feet.

He ended the kiss, releasing her slowly. Staring at him, Paige took a step back, then another and another. Without a word—what could she say after that?—she turned and hurried into the motel office.

Logan waited a moment, whether it was to give her time alone or himself time to tamp the wildness raging through him, he wasn't sure. When he did stroll into the lobby he felt at least reasonably calm and collected. He plopped down on a love seat while Paige stood at a nearby pay phone.

"Yes. Will you put me through to Ms. Regina Fox's suite, please?" he heard her say a moment later.

As tired as he was, Logan perked up at the mention of Regina Fox. What was Paige doing calling a member of one of the wealthiest families in Denver? And then he remembered the personalized tag on the car; RG ONE. So this was the lender of the sports car. Well, his damsel kept some high-cotton company. Curious, he thought. Another piece to the Paige O'Neil puzzle. Too bad he wasn't going to be around long enough to put all the pieces together. Or to do anything else with his mystery lady—

"Excuse me?" Paige said to whomever was on the other end of the conversation, her voice edged with desperation. "Oh, I see." She switched the phone from one ear to the other. "And she left no phone number where she could be reached? You're absolutely certain?" There was a long pause. "Yes, of course. Thank you."

When she didn't walk away from the phone or even turn around Logan knew something was wrong. "Problem, Rusty?" he asked, walking up to her. She didn't answer. "What's wrong?"

Finally she turned to look at him. "She isn't there," she told him, as if she didn't quite believe it.

"You can try her again in a few minutes."

"It won't do any good."

"You mean she never arrived?"

Paige shook her head. "She called from the airport and asked them to hold her room for four days."

"Well, where the hell is she?"

"Who knows? A side trip to Monaco. Visiting friends."

"Didn't she leave a number where she could be reached?"

"No."

"Well, that's pretty inconsiderate. How are you supposed to get in touch with her?"

"You don't understand, Logan." Paige ran a hand through her hair and felt like pulling it out by the roots. It wouldn't improve her situation, but it might help her frustration. "She thought I was all taken care of. On my way to a new job. Everything settled. So, she sort of tucked me to the back of her mind. That's just how Regi is."

"Sounds irresponsible, if you ask me. She's sure as hell left you in the lurch."

Frustrated and scared, not to mention that her nerves were still jangling from his kiss, Paige's temper flared. "You have no right to make snap judgments about my friends. Regi's a wonderful, generous person."

"What about her family?" he asked. "Maybe they know where to reach her."

"She doesn't have any family."

Logan vaguely recalled the Denver newspapers comparing Regina Fox to the young Onassis heir. No parents and only distant and very greedy relatives. "Oh," he said, regretting his earlier words.

"If I could just find her, everything would be all right."

"Well, that's not likely to happen tonight. So it looks like there's only one solution. You'll have to come home with me." He heard himself saying the words. He just couldn't believe it was his voice saying them.

"I can't. Logan, you've done enough. Isn't there a YWCA or a shelter I can go to?"

A wave of protectiveness hit him like a tsunami. "Oh, right. Why don't I just find you a cardboard box and a cozy alley?"

"Now you're being ridiculous," she told him, sounding more snappish than she intended.

The last ounce of Logan's patience evaporated. He wanted to grab her and shake her until her teeth rattled. Then he wanted to kiss her again. Neither would do. He couldn't leave her here and he was afraid not to. And he was too damned tired to make another decision, he decided. "Listen, Red. In about two seconds I'm walking out of here. Now, you can come with me, get a good night's sleep and tackle your problems in the morning, or start giving that cardboard box serious consideration." He turned and walked out of the motel office.

Paige hesitated for a heartbeat, then ran after him.

4

WHEN LOGAN FINALLY wheeled the bike onto the driveway of his home in Sweetwater Springs the night before, Paige had been so exhausted she had gone straight to bed, barely noticing the exterior or interior of the house. Now, as she stared out the kitchen window of the old farmhouse at a butter-yellow sunshiny day, she got her first good look at the neighborhood. She imagined this house had once been surrounded by open fields until it had to make way for progress. Even though Sweetwater Springs was a town, it was clear the town had grown from farm and ranch land. The houses along the street were mostly old, some even looked Victorian, and all were set on at least one-acre lots. She longed to put some of the houses, the patches of wildflowers scattered throughout the neighborhood, down on paper. In her haste to leave Denver, the one thing she regretted leaving was her art supplies. If she had a sketch pad she could easily spend a day at this window trying to capture some of the charm of life in Sweetwater Springs. Across the street, a man was mowing his lawn and, in the distance, she heard the occasional crack of a bat, probably from a sandlot baseball diamond. For the small

Texas town, it looked like business as usual. Life as usual.

Not a phrase she could apply to her own life for the last… Had it only been barely thirty-six hours since she'd walked in on Randal the Rat? Impossible. It felt like weeks. So much had changed in that brief span of time. She had changed.

She'd made a decision to lead her own life, free from Davenport influence. A simple decision, or at least it had started out that way, but the domino effect of her decision was mind-staggering. She'd gone from flush to flat broke. From feeling assured to feeling like a fish out of water. And the phone call she'd just completed was the cherry pit on top of her soured situation.

After reviewing her qualifications and his requirements, the owner of the gallery thought she sounded like a perfect fit to his clientele, but, of course, he couldn't hire her until he returned from his buying trip…in two weeks.

Time, she thought, had certainly become her enemy. Four days until she could reach Regi—if she was lucky and Regi didn't stage one of her city-hopping continuous parties. Two weeks until she could start earning a living for herself. Paige remembered thinking she needed time and anonymity. Well, this would teach her to be careful what she asked for, because she had it. In spades. She was stuck. Stranded. Between a rock and a hard place. Whatever euphemism she thought sounded the most palatable. And she honestly didn't know where to go from here, or what to do. The last thing she wanted was to go back home, but…better the devil you know than the one you don't?

Which brought her face-to-face with the very subject she'd been trying to ignore since she opened her eyes this morning.

Logan. His kiss. Her response.

She'd known the moment he looked at her he was going to kiss her. She could have stopped him. Instead she waited for it with breathless anticipation, telling herself, after all, it was just a simple thank-you and goodbye kiss. Except there was nothing simple about the kiss. And nothing else from this point on would be simple where Logan Walker was concerned.

She suspected his kiss would be as bold and powerful as he was, but how could she know that power would be the key to unlocking a depth of passion she didn't even know she possessed? How could she know that once unleashed, that passion could take control of her mind, maybe even her heart? The simple truth was that she had wanted Logan's kiss, and that kiss had been a deciding factor in agreeing to go with him to his home and, she was afraid, to the ends of the earth, if he asked her. But was that love at first sight, or lust?

She couldn't seem to summon enough objectivity to find the answer. Every time she tried, all she could do was feel, not think. Even now, in the cold light of day she tried to convince herself that the kiss had been a mistake. That kiss…well, it could complicate everything, change everything, at least for her. She couldn't think of him the same way she had yesterday and she was afraid she couldn't even look at him the same way. She had to put the kiss out of her mind and concentrate on the problem at hand, but it was hard.

She owed Logan over a hundred dollars and had fully expected to be able, with Regi's help, to repay him today. That prospect now looked slim. She marveled at how her perspective had changed in a day. Yesterday she'd considered a hundred dollars a relatively small sum of money. Today it seemed like a lot. And what if Logan wasn't willing to, or couldn't, wait for his money? She hadn't a clue about the size of his income or even what he did for a living. Maybe he needed the loan repaid immediately. Without Regi or the Houston job that meant she had to find some way to get the money now. Regi would vouch for her with the gallery owner, but she couldn't get a job without a social security number and identification. Both were long gone. She couldn't even deliver pizza without a driver's license. And then there was the problem of her skills, or lack thereof. She hardly thought Sweetwater Springs, Texas, would need galas planned or fundraisers and charity events organized. And certainly not for just four days.

"Not exactly overloaded in the marketable skills department," she murmured.

But she owed him more than money. He'd risked his life for her. How could she possibly repay something like that? She couldn't, and…and then on top of everything else, the kiss.

She wasn't supposed to think about that, but her mind, or was it her libido, was a traitor, because she couldn't think of much else. Not only couldn't she stop thinking about him, her imagination got involved and only made matters worse. Or better, depending on perspective. She didn't have to imagine his kiss, but it was useful when it came to taking the kiss to another level. A mental image of the two of them naked, wrapped in each other's arms and tangled bed sheets flashed across her mind. Sweaty bodies. Hot sex.

Oh yeah, wouldn't that just be a dandy addition to an already mounting list of complications? An insane idea. Strictly out of the question. She admitted she was attracted to him, but...

"Oh, don't be silly."

But silly hadn't made her heartbeat jump just now as she'd allowed her imagination to work overtime. Or her breasts tingle. And silly or not, the image didn't fade. She had to will herself to block it from her mind. She was looking for a new life, not a short, sizzling love affair. But if she was looking, she could do a lot worse than Logan Walker.

Irritated with her flight of fantasy, Paige shoved her hand into the pocket of her shorts. Her fingers curled around a bracelet, an engagement gift from Randal. A gold-and-diamond tennis bracelet, totaling three karats. She'd completely forgotten about it until this morning when she found it tucked into her makeup bag for safekeeping. She'd put it there, planning on wearing it during the honeymoon. While her conscience told her it actually belonged to Ran-

dal and she should send it back, reality told her it
was sheer luck the roadside thieves hadn't
searched her luggage and found it. Paige decided it was providence and it certainly met a
need.

Hopefully, Logan would hold the jewelry, easily worth ten times what she owed him, until she
could reach Regi. A barter, she thought. The
bracelet against her debt, plus room and board
for four days. The system had worked well for
several hundred years before money came along
and she didn't see any reason why Logan would
object. And if he did? Honestly, she didn't know
what she was going to do.

Paige glanced around the kitchen. After all
he'd done, the least she could do was make his
breakfast. She wasn't all that handy in front of a
stove, but scrambled eggs and bacon weren't exactly gourmet cuisine and it would keep her
mind off…other things, if there was food in the
house, that is. Determined to show her appreciation in even a small way, she went to the refrigerator and pulled out the few provisions they'd
picked up at a convenience store before they'd
arrived at Logan's house. A few moments later
while strips of country bacon were sizzling in a
cast-iron skillet, Paige wondered who had
stocked the refrigerator and pantry since Logan
had been away. Probably a friend. A female
friend, she wondered?

The tantalizing aroma of bacon frying coaxed
Logan slowly from a deep sleep. When he finally
came fully awake, the first thought through his
mind was, who the hell was in his kitchen? He

was halfway out of bed and reaching for his jeans before he realized he wasn't in his Denver apartment.

He was in Sweetwater Springs. In his grandmother's house. His house now that she was gone, but he still thought of it as Mimi's and probably always would. And he wasn't alone. Obviously, Paige was making breakfast.

Relieved, he fell back onto the bed.

Paige O'Neil, of the roadside rescue. Paige the puzzle. He'd practically bullied her into coming home with him. No practically about it, he thought, but there really hadn't been any other logical course of action. The idea of leaving her in a YWCA or a shelter was ludicrous. A cream puff like the duchess? Not a chance. She'd probably have been so nervous and scared she wouldn't have slept a wink. Then she'd have looked like hell by the time she made her interview and ended up losing the job. No, bringing her home with him had definitely been the best thing to do.

For her, or for you? his conscience whispered.

There were times, like now, Logan wished he could turn off his need to have all the questions answered, particularly when he was the subject. All right, he thought, time to look at this for what it was.

Lust. Sex. A roll in the hay. No matter how he phrased it, he wanted Paige. And after kissing her he couldn't seem to think of anything else. Not that the idea of a one-night stand wasn't appealing, but it wasn't in his plan. And neither was she. Sure, a quick, wild fling with a working man might turn her on. But only temporarily. She was a bad risk as far as he was concerned for two reasons: Regardless of the fact that she was trying to start a new life, he was positive she came from money, and sooner or later she'd go back to it. The best of intentions notwithstanding, money was a powerful magnet. And he gave Paige the benefit of the doubt. She'd been living Murphy's Law ever since he'd laid eyes on her and she'd been determined not to give in to that fear. He liked that. She'd basically had the rug jerked out from under her and he admired her for not throwing in the towel. She had certainly been frustrated enough to do exactly that. He liked that, too. Come to think of it, there were a lot of things he liked about Paige. Not the least of which were those incredible legs of hers.

Logan sighed. Which brought him to the second reason she was a bad risk: She'd sent his hormones into a spin a champion bull rider couldn't handle. And if she was going to be around for very long, he would probably do his dead-level best to get her into his bed. But she wasn't and that was that. And it was a good thing. Even if a couple of nights of incredible, hot sex—and he knew it would be both—might tame the testosterone storm whipping his body, it wouldn't change the fact that he didn't want a woman in his life, even briefly. There had only been one woman he could truly trust—his grandmother.

He sat up, swung his feet to the floor and looked around the room that had been his since the first day he came to live with Mimi. It hadn't changed much, but then neither had the rest of the house. At his insistence, she'd finally allowed a few bits of modern technology such as cable TV and a washer and dryer to replace her twenty-seven-year-old appliances. Logan smiled to himself. She'd given in, but he'd had a battle on his hands. His compassionate and soft-spoken grandmother believed soft living ruined the body and wasted the mind. She lived her life by the Ten Commandments and raised her only grandchild on those principles. And she made sure he didn't just attend Sunday school, but learned the lessons. Like any other loving grandparent, Mimi indulged his youthful exuberance, but she also doled out punishment without hesitation when he crossed the boys-will-be-boys line. It was her stories about his grandfather's years as a Texas Ranger that kindled his desire to go into law enforcement and Mimi had encouraged him despite the danger. She had been his rock and not a day passed that he didn't miss her desperately. He hadn't been certain how he'd feel living in this house again without her, but it felt good to be home. It felt right.

His stomach growled a response to the call of the delicious smells drifting up from the kitchen, pulling him from his thoughts. He got out of bed and stepped into his jeans. Paige was downstairs in the kitchen and, for reasons he couldn't explain, that felt right too.

She was standing at the stove, her back to him and he couldn't resist taking a minute to appreciate the view. His baggy jeans had been replaced by the shorts outfit that had first brought her legs to his attention. World-class legs. No question about it.

"Mornin'," he said, from the kitchen doorway.

Paige jumped at the sound of his voice, dropping the egg she had in her hand. "You scared me to death. And look what you made me do."

Logan yawned. "Sorry, Rusty. You'll find paper towels under—"

"I've already found them," she informed him, going down on her hands and knees to clean up the broken egg.

He sniffed the air. "Smells like you found the coffee, too."

"On the stove."

Logan raised one eyebrow. His house guest was obviously not a morning person. "You get up on the wrong side of the bed?" he asked, claiming a mug from the cupboard and filling it with coffee.

Paige stood up, reached for a tea towel and wiped her hands. "Sorry. You startled me. And I didn't get much sleep last night. Or the night before, come to think of it." Fortunately for her, she had always been able to function well on very little sleep.

He noticed her nervously twisting a corner of the towel. "How much?"

"A couple of hours, I think."

"Bed too lumpy?"

"No. I—I was worried about…everything."

"And all you accomplished was losing sleep."

"Yes and no. I called the airline before sunrise to check on flights. Then I tried Regi again. Not that any of it did any good. Oh, by the way…"

She dug into the left-hand pocket of her shorts. "Here's your calling card," she said, laying it on the counter.

Another side effect of his hormones. He hadn't realized she hadn't returned it last night. "Thanks," he said, picking up the card and slipping it into his back pocket. He walked to the table and sat down. "I take it ol' Regi is still out and about."

She nodded, cracking a fresh egg into a bowl. "I also called the gallery as soon as it opened at nine o'clock." She added another egg then began beating them with a fork. "Oh, that reminds me; you had a call. I didn't know if you wanted me to answer it or not so I let the machine get it. Some man named Rick, I think."

"Thanks." Logan glanced at the eight-day clock that had been sitting on the exact same place on his grandmother's hutch since he was a boy. It read nine-thirty. She must have finished her call to the gallery within the last few minutes. And if the circles under her eyes and her clipped speech were any indication she must have tied herself into a real big bundle of nerves by the time she called Houston. He sipped his coffee. "So, what did they say?"

She just kept beating the eggs as if that was the most important thing in the world.

"Rusty?"

She stopped whipping, turned toward him slightly, but didn't face him. "The owner was very nice and after talking with me he said he thought I was just the kind of person he was looking for."

"Well, that's great—"

"Unfortunately, he's flying to London today, then to Paris and on to Rome on a buying trip. So, he set up an appointment to meet with me when he returns to Houston…in two weeks."

She said it matter-of-factly, but he could have sworn her voice quivered on the last couple of words. Abruptly, she turned back to the stove, poured the eggs into the frying pan and started scrambling. If he were a gambling man, Logan would bet his next retainer that she was trying like hell not to cry. And trying to figure out what she could say to relieve him of any more obligation and make herself feel less desperate. As he watched, she dished up the finished eggs, added the bacon and a couple of slices of toast, then holding the plate with one hand, used a paper towel to wipe the stove clean where the bacon had splattered.

She set the plate of food down in front of him. "I didn't ask, but I hope you like your bacon crisp."

"It's…fine. It looks great."

"More coffee?"

"Please." The news about the Houston job was a real blow, putting her back at square one. He figured she was close to the end of her rope, if not there, holding herself together with spit and bailing wire. Sure enough he saw her hand shake as she refilled his cup then poured one for herself. Then she took a deep breath and squared her shoulders. Gutsy. He quickly looked away as she walked back to the table and sat down across from him.

"Aren't you eating?" he asked.

"I'm not hungry."

"What about your coffee?" He nodded to the full cup she'd left sitting on the counter.

"Oh. Don't wait on me," she told him. "Go ahead before it gets cold."

Logan was starving and didn't have to be told twice. He all but attacked his breakfast. "This is good. Eggs are just the way I like them. You know, you didn't have to fix breakfast, but I'm sure glad—"

"Yes, I did." She picked up her cup, but leaned against the counter instead of coming back to the table. "It's the least I could do after everything you've done."

He watched her toying with the handle of her cup, her slender fingers nervously rubbing one spot. She was trying to get up enough nerve to tell him something, or ask him something. And instinctively he knew it wasn't for more money. If she'd been willing to sleep in a shelter rather than ask for the price of a room she wouldn't ask for another nickel. But he also knew her pride wouldn't allow her to ignore the matter of payment of her loan.

"I don't like owing anyone money."

"Neither do I." They did have pride in common.

"So, I think I've come up with a way to repay you now without waiting for Regi. Maybe not in the way you expected. What I have in mind is, uh, a barter."

It was then he realized she hadn't made eye contact since he walked into the room. She didn't

want to look him in the eye. He was enough of a
student of human nature to recognize avoidance
and that it was usually connected to anger, guilt
or shame. She didn't sound angry. She'd had no
control over the car breaking down and no reason to feel guilty he could see. That left shame.
She'd done nothing to be ashamed of...yet.

The idea came to him, possibly with a little
help from his high testosterone level, that she
was about to make him an offer he couldn't refuse. An offer using the oldest form of barter between a man and a woman. She wouldn't have a
job for at least two weeks. She couldn't or
wouldn't, for whatever reason, turn to her family
for help. She had no money and wouldn't until
she could reach her friend. How was she going
to eat? Where was she going to live for four days
or possibly two weeks? And how was she going
to pay for anything?

While his rational mind rejected such an un-
orthodox proposition as offering herself, it didn't
take long for him to warm to the idea. In fact, the
more he thought about it, the warmer he got. "A
barter, huh?"

"Yes. I...give you something in exchange for
my debt."

"Not money, but something...valuable?"

Paige frowned. He was looking at her oddly.
"Yes. It should cover my debt plus room and
board for four days."

"Don't forget nights."

"Of course. And I want you to know up front
that..." He got up from the table and slowly
came toward her in a way that made her think of

a predatory animal. "...that you're not, uh...obligated to do it." He stopped less than two feet away, his gaze so intense she felt it like a physical touch. Then his gaze went to her mouth. Paige blinked, flashing back to her earlier image of sweaty bodies and hot sex. It was as if he was aiming all of that primitive sensuality directly at her—and, at this range, it was lethal.

"Now, why," he said, softly, "would you think I'd say no to such a proposition?"

"Well, b-because you haven't heard...all the—" her breath caught when he traced the curve of her jaw up to her earlobe, then ran his finger around the diamond studs in her ear "—particulars."

"I've heard it called a lot of things, but never that. But then a rose by any other name..." He leaned forward, almost nuzzling her neck. "Speaking of roses, you sure smell good. What is that?"

"J-joy."

"I'll say." He drew back and looked into her eyes. "So, when did you want to consummate this barter?"

Consummate? What a strange way of putting it. Suddenly, the lightbulb in her head clicked on. Nights? Proposition? "Wait a minute." She put a hand on his chest. "Are we talking about the same thing?"

"What I can't figure out is why we're talking at all when there's a great big ol' bed right up those stairs."

Ohmygod!

"You're talking about…you think I'm offering…myself?" she asked, stunned.

"Well, it's not like it hasn't been done before."

She shifted to the right, moving away from him. "Not by me it hasn't."

Logan frowned. "What's going on? You just offered to—"

"No, I didn't." She continued to moved away. He followed her. "But you said—"

"I said I was interested in a barter, not a brothel," she said, gazing at him stonily. "Naturally, being a man, that's all you thought I had to offer. Well, it's not."

She reached into her pocket, pulled out the bracelet and placed it on the counter beside him. Logan blinked. "What's that?"

"A gold-and-diamond bracelet."

"I can see that, but why are you giving it to me?"

"*This* is what I'm offering as collateral until I can get your money," she explained. "And I can guarantee you it's worth several times what I owe."

Logan stared at the piece of jewelry, the row of diamonds winking in the morning sunlight. He was thinking hot sex and she offered cold rocks. A little too quick out of the chute, and the wrong chute at that. And why?

Try wish fulfillment.

He'd jumped to the wrong conclusion because he'd been thinking about getting her in bed practically from the first moment they met. He didn't want a trinket, dammit. He wanted her. He'd let his hormones overload his good sense, and look where it had gotten him? Looking like a prize jackass.

He picked up the bracelet, resisting the urge to throw it in the trash. "Where'd you get this?" he snapped.

"It was a gift."

"From a lover?" His wounded ego was talking now. He knew it, but couldn't seem to stop it. Anger reared its ugly head, pricking his better judgment like a devil with a pitchfork. She'd made a fool out of him. No, he'd been a fool to ever think she could step out of her ivory tower for a little fun with a plain ordinary, working-class guy.

"Does it make any difference?"

It did to Logan. He didn't like the idea that she had been close enough to another man to accept a hunk of sparkle like the one he was holding. The way he felt at the moment he was tempted to take it all right. Take a hammer to it.

"Where?"

She raised her chin, meeting his gaze directly. "A former fiancé."

"How former?" He knew it was none of his business, but he had to know.

"If you must know, as of two days ago."

"Damned convenient. Too bad you didn't come up with this yesterday. You could have hocked it and gone back to your rich friends instead of riding on the back of a motorcycle. But I doubt you'd have gotten more than a fourth of what it's worth."

"I—I never thought about pawning it," she said. Probably because she'd never really felt it was hers. She still didn't, but she wanted to let him know that she wasn't just taking advantage of his kindness. She paid her debts—but not with sex.

Very deliberately Logan laid the bracelet on the counter. "No, thanks. Not interested."

"Excuse me?" she said, shocked at his curt dismissal of her idea.

"You heard me."

"Yes, but…" Paige stopped herself. She wouldn't beg, no matter how disappointed she was. "All right, if that's how you feel."

"It is. But if you're just dying to barter, I've got a suggestion."

"And that is?"

"A job."

"I don't understand."

"I'm offering you a job. Cleaning, cooking, doing the marketing, laundry. You know, the usual housekeeping chores."

"You want me to be your maid?"

"Basically. Obviously, you can cook. And the rest is pretty simple stuff. Tell you what," he said, feeling a little ruthless. His saner self knew he would pay a price for being a bully, but ego was in the driver's seat, and it was hell on wheels. "You owe me a hundred and change, so we'll say a fifty a week. That'll cover you until your fancy gallery person returns. And if your friend turns up in Paris before then, you'll be able to pay me off."

She looked at him for a second as if trying to decide whether to burst into tears or spit in his eye. She did neither. Very calmly, she walked over to the coffeepot and refilled her cup. "And for cleaning this house you're willing to cancel my debt?"

"You'll earn it, Red. This house hasn't been lived in on a regular basis for more than a year. There's enough dusting alone to keep you busy for two days."

Paige refused to give him the satisfaction of seeing her unnerved. She'd bluff her way through this if it took every ounce of her control. And it just might. "A year? I—I thought this was your home."

"Hometown."

"Then where do you live?"

"Denver."

Paige's eyes widened. "D-Denver?" She couldn't believe it. Here she was, no money, no friends, stuck with an ex-cop who bartered for housecleaning and sex, and now she'd discovered he was from Denver, no less. It was too much. Could her luck get any worse?

"Got something against Denver?" he asked.

"What? No. I, uh… No."

"Got something against hard work?"

"Of course not."

"Then do we have a deal?"

She could tell by the look in his eyes he didn't think she could do it. Hide and watch, she thought, squaring her shoulders. "Absolutely." She took a step forward, but he was in her way. "Excuse me," she said. When he stepped aside, she picked up the bracelet, slipped it in her pocket, then pointed at his plate. "Are you done?"

"Yeah, I'm done."

She stacked the plate and cups, carried them to the sink and began cleaning up.

"I'm—I'll be outside scraping paint if you need…" He'd almost said "me," but decided it might be misunderstood. "….if you need anything."

"Fine."

Logan stalked out of the kitchen, more than a little disgusted with himself for losing his cool over that damned bracelet. So she was somebody's ex-fiancée. So what? So some other man, a rich man, had given her diamonds and gold. So what? It wasn't like they had a thing going. She'd offered the jewelry in a fair exchange.

And he had refused.

Which was his right. Of course, that remark about hocking the bracelet for a fourth of its value was nothing more than a guess. A wild one at that. The truth was she'd nicked his pride, he'd lost his temper and, as usual when that happened, he wound up in a messy situation. And while he was dishing out the truth, he might as well admit to wanting a little of his own back, or he would never have suggested the job as housekeeper. A maid for crying out loud. What had he been thinking?

He'd been thinking about getting her between the sheets, and not much else. He wanted her so bad he could taste it.

And dammit all to hell, she'd turned him down.

Not that he didn't deserve it.

What he'd done was downright mean, and

that wasn't like him. Which only proved his point. Paige O'Neil had him tied in more knots than a sailor ever thought about. He'd been close to ravishing her delectable body not two seconds after he thought she was making him a tasty offer. Well, this was a helluva mess. He should be ashamed of himself. And he was. A little.

Thank goodness he only had to stay in control of his baser instincts for four days. He could last for a few more days.

That's what he'd thought about the four miles, and look where he was now.

5

PAIGE STOOD IN the open door to the utility room staring at an unfamiliar and, from her point of view, hostile environment. Washer, dryer, bucket, mop, broom and a vacuum cleaner. She was relieved Logan had gone into Lubbock to pick up paint for the outside of the house because she'd just as soon he wasn't around if she made a total mess of things and ended up looking like a fool. Particularly since she had neglected to inform him of one minor detail concerning their deal. Well, two actually.

Her housecleaning experience was minimal to nonexistent.

And the only thing she knew how to cook was bacon and eggs.

The cleaning, she decided optimistically, was a matter of common sense. The cooking was simply a matter of reading a cookbook and following instructions. She didn't intend to fall down on her end of the deal.

Their deal. She hadn't been prepared for the way it turned out. And she certainly hadn't been prepared for the mistaken conclusion he'd come to that she was offering herself to him. Shocked? Yes, she'd definitely been shocked. And...

And secretly thrilled.

She wouldn't be human if she didn't admit a part of her had been flattered that he'd not only have gone along with such an idea, but actually seemed pleased about it. And, to be fair, she admitted thoughts of having sex with Logan were popping up with increasing regularity, but it would be a mistake to let their deal get out of hand, so to speak. Probably.

Paige sighed, coming back to the more immediate problem. Namely, the cleaning. "A deal is a deal," she said, resigned to make the best of the situation.

Searching for rags and cleaning products, she opened a cabinet and found everything from toilet bowl scrub to furniture polish. Funny, she thought, they all looked alike. All were in plastic bottles and almost all of the labels claimed pine tree extracts—Pine-All, Pino-Whiz, Deluxe Pine Oil—and promised nearly miraculous results. After plopping four or five bottles into the bucket, she picked up the mop and went into the kitchen. Earlier, accompanied by the strains of country music from a portable radio, she'd swept the floor, but afterward it didn't shine the way the kitchen floor at home did. So, she decided, it must need mopping.

After lining the cleaning products up on the counter beside the sink, she turned the bottles, labels facing the wall, and began reading instructions. One was multipurpose, a couple specifically for bathrooms, one for polishing only, and almost all had to be diluted. Paige decided on the multipurpose product. And if one-fourth cup cleaner to one gallon of water was adequate, then surely one whole cup to one gallon would clean that much better. She stuck the bucket under the tap and turned on the water. While the bucket filled she picked up what she thought was the multipurpose cleaner, measured out a cup and added it to the water. She cranked the volume on the radio, filling the room with Garth Brooks singing about his friends in low places as she set her pace to the beat. Thirty minutes later she had mopped half the kitchen floor and turned to admire her handiwork.

Paige frowned. Part of the floor had dried, but the part that was still wet looked spotted, as if the cleaner had formed beads that were too thick to dry evenly. The cleaner must be old, she thought, remembering the house wasn't lived in regularly. Well, she would just have to work a little harder. But no matter how many passes she made with the mop, a thin layer of cleaner stayed on the floor.

It simply refused to dry. And it was slick.

After an hour bent over the handle of a mop, working as diligently as she knew how, Paige realized all she had gained was an aching back and, if possible, a bigger problem than she'd had in the beginning. There was almost no water on the floor, but it was still slick. Great. The first project she'd tackled and she'd made one huge mess of it. Frustrated, she went back to recheck the instructions, hoping they contained an "if this happens, do this" paragraph. As she picked up the bottle she saw the label, Deluxe Pine Oil.

Pine oil!

Oh, no. Half of the kitchen floor was coated

with furniture polish! Lord, no wonder it was slick. How in the world was she going to get pine oil off a linoleum floor? And what if Logan came home and saw what a colossal mess she'd made of things?

Don't panic, she told herself, then decided panic was a great motivator.

As fast as she could, Paige went back to the utility room, rummaged through the cabinets until she found a scrub brush. Returning to the kitchen she grabbed the multipurpose cleaner, making sure she got the right one this time, mixed some with water and began scrubbing the floor. She was about a third of the way finished when the back door banged open and Logan strode into the kitchen with a brown paper bag in one hand and a handled six-pack carton of beer in the other.

"No, Logan! Wait—"

His feet flew out from under him before she could finish her warning and he landed with a thud. The brown bag hit the floor and ripped, spilling cantaloupes. When she saw the beer about to fall Paige flung her body over the floor like a runner sliding into home plate. Luckily, the carton dropped, fell over and the bottles rolled across the floor, their amber bodies rocking in the puddled water like downed bowling pins. But in her desperate attempt to save the beer, she kicked over the bucket, spilling dirty mop water everywhere

"What the hell happened?" Logan asked, sitting up.

"I tried to warn you," Paige told him, crawling

across the slippery linoleum to him, "but you were already—"

"On my ass. Yeah, I know." He glanced around, noticing the overturned bucket. "What were you doing? Trying to flood the house?" He reached up and touched the back of his head. "Ouch. Damn."

Without thinking, Paige scrambled up beside him and plowed her hands through his hair feeling for bumps. "Oh, God. I'll never forgive myself if you're hurt."

"I don't think—"

"Does you head hurt?"

"Well, sure—"

"Is your vision blurred?"

"Rusty." He took her hands from his hair. "I'm not hurt. But you're a mess," he told her, eyeing her clothes.

She looked down. The front of her shirt and shorts were soaked with dirty water. "Oh, yuk."

"Don't look now, but you're sitting in it." He glanced down. "As a matter of fact, so am I."

"Oh, I'm so sorry. I wanted to have this all finished before you got home and now…" She fought the riptide of emotion threatening to pull her under, but it was too strong. "Oh-h, no…" She was going to cry and she hated it.

He'd stayed gone until he could get up the nerve to apologize for his anger, and now her tears shot what courage he'd managed to find all to hell. He had to snap her out of this before she flooded the place. More than it already was. "C'mon, Rusty, don't fold on me now."

"Fold?" Swiping at the river of tears, she

shoved a mass of hair away from her cheek only to discover it too was wet. How dare he manipulate her into cleaning his damned house then say something like that. She knew she wasn't thinking reasonably, and didn't care. "In the last twenty-four hours I've faced robbery and the possibility of rape without shedding a tear. You think I'll fold now?"

"Rusty—"

"You'd like that, wouldn't you?"

"Rusty—"

"You'd like nothing better than to see me sitting in this puddle of mop water blubbering like a baby. Not a chance," she told him, hating that she was doing precisely that. She had to get out, get away from him.

When she tried to get up, Logan grabbed her by the arm, pulling her back down. And instantly knew he'd made a mistake by touching her. All the anger and sexual frustration, plus her earlier rejection exploded in him, bursting into white-hot passion. And before he knew what he was doing, his mouth took hers. His kiss was hard and deep. Hot and wild.

It was all there, everything she wanted and had tried to deny. All the heat and power she'd sensed in him from the beginning. It emanated off him in waves and she didn't even try to resist. He leaned closer, tilting her head back as he slanted his lips firmly over hers. He seduced her with his mouth, coaxing, arousing and demanding until she was mindless with need. Clutching his shirt, she leaned into the kiss, making a soft little sound, eloquently expressing that need. In response, he crushed her against the hard wall of his chest and took the kiss deeper. Pleasure, overwhelming pleasure, rippled through her body creating an almost unbearable tension and she moaned her satisfaction.

Leaning back, he took her with him until she was sprawled on top of him. Then, one hand holding her head for his ravenous kiss, the other slid down her body, pausing to stroke the side of her breast before moving on to cup her fanny and press her hips to his arousal. He was a heartbeat away from rolling her beneath him and ripping her clothes off when...

The back door flew open followed by the sound of boots stomping over linoleum. "Hey, Walker. Word's out you're back and the town's hidin' their beer and women."

Startled, Logan and Paige looked up, then quickly rolled away from each other.

Two tall cowboys, one with sandy-blond hair, the other dark, stopped dead in their tracks at the doorway to the kitchen and stared at the couple on the floor. Finally, after several awkward seconds, one looked at the other and grinned.

"Looks like he brought his own."

If there had been a loose piece of linoleum Paige would gladly have crawled under it. Not only was she—were they both—a mess from the wet floor, but it must look as if they'd just been doing, well...exactly what they'd been doing. She was still breathing hard and could feel her lips were swollen. They still tingled from his kiss. No doubt they were red, as was the rest of her face.

Logan, on the other hand, didn't seem the least bit embarrassed. "Well, look what the wind blew in," he said, getting to his feet. "Uh, Paige O'Neil—" he helped her up "—meet Cade McBride and Reese Barrett. Two of the most ornery, broke-down old bull riders—"

Both men immediately removed their hats. "Broke-down?" said the sandy-haired cowboy. "Did you hear that, Reese?"

"Pay no attention to him, ma'am. He never did have any manners," the other cowboy said, shaking her hand. "Reese Barrett. Pleased to meet you."

"Cade McBride. And that goes double, Ms. O'Neil." He pumped her hand.

"I, uh… Nice to meet both of you. Please excuse the mess," she said, not sure which looked the worse for wear, her or the kitchen floor.

With a knowing grin, Cade winked at Logan. "Looked like a little good clean fun to me. Sorry we interrupted."

"Yeah. We can come back later," Reese offered.

"You'll have to forgive us, ma'am, if our jaws hit the floor when we walked in. We just never thought anyone as worthless as ol' Logan here would be lucky enough to find such a beautiful woman willing to put up with him."

Paige realized Logan's friends had assumed they'd walked in on a lover's tussle. "Oh, no. It's not—"

"Not a problem at all. Don't give it another thought," Logan told them, cutting her off.

"Guess we got a little rambunctious." He nodded toward the overturned bucket.

All three men grinned and Paige didn't have to be a mind reader to know what they were thinking. She was mortified. And mad as hell. "Logan—"

"Uh, Rusty. You might want to think about changing your clothes," he reminded her.

Paige looked down at her wet shirt plastered so revealingly to her body. "Oh." She turned and rushed out of the kitchen.

Reese cleared his throat. "Sorry, buddy. Looks like you may catch hell when we leave."

"Probably."

"Why didn't you let us know you were bringing your lady with you?"

"Didn't know myself. Paige and I happened kinda sudden, you know what I mean?"

"Hey, you're preachin' to the choir. We've been there. Right, Reese?"

"You're telling me. Who'd have thought a year ago that I'd be head over heels for a sexy genius with twins on the way and loving every minute of it."

Cade glanced in the direction Paige had disappeared, then back at Logan. "Say, you didn't by any chance go off and get yourself married, did you?"

"No. And by the way, since I didn't make the wedding—" he shook hands with Reese "—or the christening—" he shook Cade's hand "—congratulations to both of you. I'd offer you each a beer to celebrate, but..." He pointed to the amber bottles on the floor. "...maybe next time."

"We'll hold you to it," Cade said. "Sorry we can't hang around and shoot the breeze but we're on our way into Lubbock. I have to pick up a new hay bailer."

"And I have to pick up Shea from the bank," Reese added. "She's been doing some consulting work for them."

"Tell you what, we'll check with our wives and maybe we can all get together for dinner. And, for sure, we're all going together to the reunion dance Saturday night, right?" Cade said.

"I don't know."

"Whatdaya mean, you don't know? Here I've been scouring the countryside tryin' to bribe some unsuspecting female into being your date and you show up with Ms. Long-Stemmed American Beauty. Nice legs, by the way."

"Damn straight." Logan grinned. "But, uh, Paige only has a couple of days left. She may not be here Saturday."

"Too bad," Reese commented.

"Yeah," Logan agreed. It was too bad. He'd forgotten about the reunion dance, but it would be nice to walk in with Paige on his arm.

"Well, check out the dinner thing with Paige— you know how women are about men making plans without asking—and we'll give you a call."

Paige was probably making plans to kill him right about now, Logan thought. "Yeah. I'll, uh, check with her and let you know."

When he'd walked his friends to the door, Cade stopped. "You know, I was beginning to think that gold digger, Cindi, had put you off marriage for good. Glad to see she didn't."

"What makes you think that?"

"The way you look at Paige."

A few moments later Cade and Reese had gone, leaving him to face his fate. An hour later, he was still waiting, but he hadn't been idle. The kitchen floor was clean and dry and so was he. Considering he hadn't heard so much as a peep out of Paige since she ran out, and he wasn't sure what to expect when she finally did come down, maybe mopping would earn him a point or two. Especially after kissing her... Kissing her? Hell, he'd all but devoured her mouth. And he wanted to do a lot more.

Logan ran a hand through his hair. He still couldn't believe how quickly the kiss had gone out of control, how quickly *he'd* gone out of control. If Cade and Reese hadn't walked in when they did, no telling what might have happened. No, he knew what would have happened. He would have made love to Paige right there on the kitchen floor. No question. But the thing that had him confused was that she had met him with equal passion, heat for heat. And what heat! He hadn't expected that. No feigned resistance before giving in to the kiss, just straightforward, honest-to-God passion. She was wildfire in his arms.

He loved it. And it scared the hell out of him.

He'd been hot after her body from the very first and told himself it was to be expected after so long of doing without, and that almost any reasonably attractive woman would have the same effect. All true as far as it went. He was most definitely still hot after her body and it certainly was to be expected after his self-imposed abstinence. But he was beginning to think a hundred women in bikinis could parade past him and none of them would have the same effect on him as Paige.

The truth was he didn't want her to leave. And he liked the idea that his friends accepted them as a couple. The only problem was getting Paige to see it that way, but he had a notion about overcoming her objection. Pride was her greatest vulnerability, and while he knew he should be ashamed to exploit weakness, he wanted her enough to be shameless. And while he was planning on being shameless he might as well throw in not telling her what he did for a living. Every instinct he had was practically screaming at him to avoid that piece of truth or she would run like a scared rabbit. And he didn't want her running anywhere but straight into his arms. No way around it. Not telling her was a lie by omission, and if his grandmother were still alive she'd warm the seat of his britches but good. That did give him a twinge of regret, but... At that moment he heard a door close upstairs.

Paige stood at the top of the stairs trying to calm her nerves with only limited success. If she hadn't been able to accomplish it in the last hour, she might as well give up. Just the thought of being in the same room with Logan again gave her goose bumps. She had never...*never* been kissed the way he had kissed her. It was like standing in the opening of a blast furnace; the heat was overwhelming, all consuming. And she had practically walked straight into the blaze without hesitation. Astounding, she thought. Before yesterday she'd never laid eyes on him and today she'd been only minutes away from making love with him. If his friends hadn't shown up when they did, she had no doubt where the kiss would have ended. And the truly strange thing was that part of her was sorry they had been interrupted. She'd been shocked and angry that he'd allowed his friends to assume the worst, but in all honesty, the assumption was correct. The instant his lips touched hers, something inside her, something she hadn't even known was there, responded. Something elemental, intense and thrilling. The question now was what did she intend to do about it? What in the world was she going to do about wanting Logan?

There was no future in wanting him, even having him. He'd made it clear he didn't want a woman in his life, particularly one who came from money or wanted money. Whoever his ex-wife was, she'd certainly poisoned his perspective where money and women were concerned. What had she done, Paige wondered, taken him for everything he had, or run off with another man with more money? Although why any woman in her right mind would choose someone else over Logan didn't make any sense to her. How could any woman look at him and not be attracted, not feel the chemistry, the aura of sexual energy?

Paige thought about that for a moment. Chemistry was a pitifully inadequate word for what she felt, but it might not be the same for Logan. A man with his looks and sheer animal magnetism probably had women whenever he wanted, however he wanted them. Not that she was a virgin, but the thought occurred to her that maybe the Davenport shackles had restricted more than her artistic ambitions. Maybe she craved another kind of freedom.

And why not?

Hadn't she denied herself excitement long enough? Come to think of it, wasn't she still? She was attracted to him, yet automatically denied it, telling herself involvement would be a mistake. The word undignified even crept into her thoughts, which was crazy. Old habits, she thought. Exactly the kind she wanted to eliminate from her life. What was the point of building a new life if all she did was drag don'ts and shouldn'ts from the old life along with her? And sex certainly fell into that category.

Randal had been an adequate lover, very caring, always making sure the pleasure was shared. On that score, at least, their relationship hadn't been dull. But his kisses had never excited her the way Logan's had. And she'd never felt the need she felt when she was with Logan. Wasn't she entitled to feel the earth move? Take a walk on the wild side, just once?

Whatever this *thing* was between them was undoubtedly short-term. She didn't expect anything other than a fling, and she certainly wasn't planning on falling in love with him. But there was nothing wrong with allowing her desire to take its natural course. And if she did, there was absolutely nothing wrong in enjoying it. The problem was she didn't consider herself a femme fatale; she wasn't sure if she should tell Logan her feelings or let him take the lead. She decided on the course of least resistance. For the time being she'd just go with the flow for a while, see which direction Logan was headed.

She walked back into the kitchen and was surprised to see the floor gleaming. "You didn't have to do this," she said, feeling guilty that she hadn't done her job.

"Yeah, I did. Guess you're ticked off, huh?"

"I was."

"Now, before you go getting yourself all riled up over nothing—"

"Logan, you embarrassed me in front of your friends just so you could look like a stud. I don't call that nothing."

"You're right. I'm sorry."

Paige had been prepared for arrogance, not surrender. "Why did you let them think we were...you know?"

"Lovers."

"Yes. Why didn't you tell them the truth?"

"Believe it or not, I hadn't planned to give them the wrong impression, but when they did it just seemed like it would be easier all the way around not to set the record straight."

"Why do you say that?"

"To begin with, there was no point in telling them it was just a harmless kiss. They could see for themselves that wasn't true. Second, in a sort of backhanded way I was protecting your reputation."

"Protecting my—"

"Now, hear me out, Rusty. Sweetwater Springs isn't stuck in the 1950s, but it isn't exactly on the cutting edge either. Folks around here like their preaching loud and their sex straight. You're looking at Middle America in boots and cowboy hats. And it's been this way practically since they invented dirt. What I'm trying to say is that, as unenlightened as it sounds, your reputation will wear better if everybody thinks we're lovers rather than an employer and employee shacked up together."

"You can't be serious."

"Cross my heart," he said, making the appropriate motions.

"But it feels…dishonest somehow."

"Any more than introducing you as my maid?" He took both of her hands in his. "Take a look, Red. Ever seen hands this smooth and soft after scrubbing toilets for a while? Or nails this well kept?"

She had to admit he had a point. "No."

"You'll be gone in a few days." He shrugged. "No harm, no foul. So, I figured it would be easier if they thought you're my lady. Particularly after them walking in on us. But just because I thought I was protecting your honor, so to speak, doesn't make it all right. I'll set them straight. In fact, I'll call them now if you want me to."

"That's not necessary." He was still holding her hands and she felt the tingle of energy all the way to her shoulder. "You can tell them after I'm gone."

"Yeah," he said, gazing at her with that hungry look. "I can, but—"

A pounding on the back door interrupted him. "Hey, we're knocking this time."

A second later Cade walked in with Reese a step behind. As they removed their hats, Cade announced, "This is a kidnapping. Hey, Paige. Good to see you again."

Logan looked at his friends as if they'd lost their minds. "How much beer you guys had since you left here?"

"We don't usually drink until after we abduct. Right?" Cade said to Reese.

"Beats me. This is my first kidnapping."

"What the hell are you talking about?" Logan asked.

"The wives have given the word, cowboy. We're to bring the two of you to the ranch for dinner. Steaks are marinatin' even as we speak, and Belle has already given Posey orders for her homemade tortillas and salsa. How about it, Paige?"

"I—I." She didn't know how to respond other than stare and stutter.

"Why you dog," Reese accused, "from the look on the poor girl's face I'll bet you didn't even mention all of us having dinner together sooner or later."

"I didn't know you meant tonight."

"Just turned out to be sooner than later."

"Thanks," Logan said. "But I don't think—"

"Why don't we let Paige decide." And they all turned to her.

"Well, I—I didn't bring a lot of clothes with

me," she told them, knowing she was taking a step down the wild side. "I'm not sure what to wear."

"If you don't mind me saying so, ma'am," said the soft-spoken Reese, "you look fine just like you are."

"Damn straight," Cade agreed. "Trust me, we go for comfort. What you see is what you'll get. And I promise my wife will be in something similar to what you're wearing only without shoes."

"Well, I…" She looked at Logan who was still staring at her.

"We're not takin' no for an answer." Cade slapped Logan's shoulder with his hat. "If I don't see that motorcycle in my rearview mirror I'll just have to come back and get you." Then he and Reese walked out the door.

"Why didn't you tell them the truth?" Logan asked, as soon as they were out of earshot.

"It was a harmless…misinterpretation, I guess you could call it. As you pointed out, I'll only be here for a few days, and it wasn't as if you set out to deliberately lie to your friends."

"The result was the same."

"Yes, but you said you'd make it right after I'm gone, and I think you'll honor that."

Logan couldn't help but grin. She was making his argument for him. "You sure are trusting."

"And I'm trying to let you off the hook, here. Do you want off or don't you?"

"Absolutely, and I'm mighty appreciative." He paused, then since she seemed to be in a forgiving mood, decided to go for broke. "Considering this day has been downright busting at the

seams with wrong conclusions—first me, then
my friends—and if you add what happened before Cade and Reese showed up the first time, I
figured—"

"Oh…that."

"Yeah, that. I half-expected you to be mad because I kissed you."

"How could I be? I kissed you back, didn't I?"

"Yes, ma'am," he said, drawing the word out
softly, like a caress. "You surely did."

"Well, we would, uh, really be dishonest if we
tried to pretend it hadn't happened, or that it
wasn't…" He was looking at her with that same
intensity he had before he kissed her the first
time. It was like looking into a blue flame. And to
think she'd once thought that she didn't even
care about the color of his eyes. Paige cleared her
throat. "Anyway, I don't see any harm in joining
your friends for dinner."

"No harm at all. And I promise, you'll have a
nice time." He didn't completely understand
why she had gone along with him, despite the
reasons he'd presented. But he didn't care. She
was his for tonight, at least.

6

As they followed Cade's pickup truck, the sun was barely above the horizon, filling the sky with a blaze of color that made Paige long for a sketch pad. She'd seen thousands of sunsets but she couldn't remember one that had filled her with such awe and inspiration. Maybe it had something to do with not seeing it through a bay window or through the windshield of a car, but experiencing it. The color and beauty surrounded her like a blanket of rainbows. When Logan turned the bike into the driveway of the McBride ranch, putting the view behind them, she was sorry they couldn't keep riding straight into the sunset. He swung around to the side of the house, parked beside Cade's truck, killed the engine and helped Paige off.

"I heard you coming from a mile a way."

Paige glanced up to see Cade coming down the patio steps with a stunningly beautiful dark-haired woman on his arm. The woman had a baby on her hip.

"Paige O'Neil," Cade said. "This is my wife, Belle."

"Nice to meet you," she said.

"And this handsome devil—" he chucked the ba-by under the chin "—is our son, Chance." As if he knew he was the center of attention, the baby grinned, displaying two gleaming teeth, one up, one down.

"He's beautiful," Paige said.

"Thanks." Belle smiled. "We're glad you could make it. Shea should be here any minute." Belle had no sooner made the statement than a Suburban rolled to a stop behind Logan's bike. Reese got out, then went over and opened the door. A few seconds later a petite and decidedly pregnant woman slid out of the front seat. Her husband was on hand to steady her descent and offer assistance as they walked to join everyone.

"Shea, I'd like you to meet Logan Walker and Paige O'Neil. My wife, Shea," Reese said, finishing the introductions.

Handshakes and greetings went all around.

"I don't know about the rest of you," Cade said, "but I'm starving."

Shea looked at her husband. "Same goes for me, cowboy."

"And we don't stand on ceremony," Belle pointed out. "So, feel free to ask for what you want."

"What I want is a crane," Shea said. "It sure would make getting up those steps easier."

"No problem, Bright Eyes." And with that Reese Barrett scooped his wife into his arms and carried her up the flight of stairs to the flagstone patio.

"Show-off," Cade commented and they all laughed.

Within thirty minutes Paige felt as if she'd known Logan's friends for years. She'd never been around a more loving and relaxed group of people. They all teased each other, especially the men. But the woman gave as good as they got. As an only child, Paige imagined this was what it might feel like to have brothers and sisters. Except for Logan, of course. She certainly didn't think of him in brotherly terms.

As she watched the three male friends it was clear their friendship was as long-standing and solid as the State of Texas. Exceptional men. All of them tall, broad-shouldered, well built and just plain gorgeous. And as if that weren't enough, each had special "added attractions." Cade had a quick smile and an easy laugh. Reese had a quiet strength, a calm spirit.

And then there was Logan.

Logan with all that intensity and sensuality. All that power that seemed to be held in check, but just barely, like the engine of his bike idling, waiting for the touch of the rider's hands. He was definitely the handsomest, sexiest of the three. Of course, her opinion might be biased. Particularly since she'd glanced up once or twice to find him looking at her with enough heat in his eyes to reduce the size of the polar ice cap. And, every time, her body responded instantly. Her pulse quickened and so did her blood.

When the steaks were ready, all six sat at a huge round table set with little Chance in his high chair between his mother and father. The food was delicious, the conversation light and lively.

"So, Paige," Cade asked, feeding Chance a bite of watermelon, "how in the world did a smart, good-looking lady like you have the bad luck to wind up with Walker here?"

She glanced at Logan, trying to gauge his re-action, but he seemed perfectly calm. "I think I was attracted to the Harley first," she answered, remembering his daring rescue.

Reese leaned around Shea, looking at Cade. "Told you we needed to get one of those."

"Easy, cowboy," she warned. "The only wheels in your future will be on tricycles."

"Paige and I sort of met by accident." Logan jumped in hoping to steer the conversation away from specifics. "She had car trouble, and I gave her a ride."

Cade grinned. "Aw, shucks. A hero."

"Stuff it, McBride."

"Behave boys," Belle ordered then directed her attention to Paige. "I thought you might have met through one of Logan's cas—"

"Darlin'," Cade interrupted his wife, "would you pass me some of those tortillas?"

Belle gave him a strange look as she handed him the container of hot tortillas. "What kind of work do you do, Paige?"

"I teach art to underprivileged children," she said, receiving a round of enthusiastic responses.

"No, kiddin'?"

"That's great."

"How wonderful."

"I'm impressed."

And one surprised look.

"At least, I did," she amended. "I had to leave my old job for a new one in Houston. The salary is much better, but the main reason I'm taking it is that I'll also be in charge of an annual festival that promotes local artists with the proceeds going toward scholarships for kids. My dream is to someday open an art school for underprivileged children."

"Good for you," Belle said. "I bet you'll do it, too."

"Do you have a lot experience organizing events?" Shea asked.

"Some." There were times when Paige had felt like her whole life was one big charity event after another and she was on practically every committee. The only thing that made it tolerable was that she knew she was helping others through the work.

"I wish you were going to be around long enough to give Belle and I a few pointers on our little craft fair. We volunteered thinking it would be a snap, but it didn't take us long to discover we were both in over our heads."

"Are we ever," Belle agreed. "And I hate that you may not be here for the reunion dance Saturday night. It would have been fun for the six of us to go together."

"Reunion? What reunion?" She glanced at Logan and saw him frown.

"The Sweetwater Springs High School reunion." Belle looked at Paige. "Didn't Logan tell you? It's been fifteen years since these three graduated. Although, judging from what Cade's told me, I suspect they gave them diplomas just to get them out of the principal's hair. And his office."

"I don't know anything about a reunion or a dance."

Both women looked at Logan. "You should be ashamed—" Shea began but Belle stopped her.

"Oh, let me." Belle's smile was deceptively sweet. "I've known him just long enough to be mean."

"Hang on to your hat, Walker," Cade warned.

"You *should* be ashamed of yourself for not telling her. You don't just spring that kind of thing on a woman at the last minute."

"Gimme a break, Belle. Paige is only gonna be here for a couple more days. I didn't want her to feel bad because she couldn't make the dance."

"Oh, and I suppose you think that little bit of chivalry lets you off the hook."

"Obviously not. But I'd forgotten about it myself until Cade said something about it this afternoon."

"A likely excuse," Shea said, but she was smiling.

"C'mon, Bright Eyes." Her husband insisted, pulling her out of her chair. "Let the poor guy off the hook and let's you and me trip the light fantastic."

Shea laughed. "If you're thinking 'light' you've got the wrong woman. Don't say you weren't warned," she told him, moving into his arms.

Little Chance, who had been amazingly sweet natured all evening, evidently decided he wasn't getting enough of his parents' attention and began playing a game of drop the bunny. He dropped the stuffed animal or threw it off his high chair and Mom or Dad retrieved it, then Chance started the whole process over again. And all three were having a great time.

Paige sighed. She liked these people a lot. Maybe more than she'd liked anyone in a long time, and she hated the thought that they would soon learn she had enjoyed their hospitality and friendship under false pretenses. And the more she thought about it, the more she wanted to tell them the truth. But she wouldn't, because it might embarrass Logan. And to be honest, even though she'd never see these people again she didn't want them to think badly of her. And while she was being honest, she was uneasy with the lie for another reason.

She wished it were true.

That's why she didn't let Logan tell the truth about their relationship. That's why she had decided to be with him.

Don't do this, she told herself. One kiss, no matter how hot, didn't mean anything but a kiss. And when it came right down to it, neither would one night, no matter how passionate. And a night with Logan would be passionate. Wild and erotic beyond her wildest dreams. And while those dreams might be wonderfully, deliciously fulfilled, and she would have her walk on the wild side, for the first time she wondered how she might feel afterward. Could she keep it to just a brief affair? Yes, she would have to, because something told her Logan Walker was the kind of man who left scars on a woman's heart if she made the fatal mistake of falling for him.

The soft strains of a country waltz tugged her

out of her thoughts and she watched as Reese danced with Shea, the two of them as close as her tummy would permit. Suddenly realizing Logan was standing beside her, she looked up and almost caught her breath, he was so handsome. He smiled and held out his hand.

"How 'bout a dance?"

"Yes, I'd love to."

"Sorry about that reunion thing," he said, swinging her into his arms. "Hope you weren't embarrassed."

"Not, too," she lied.

They danced in silence for a moment before he said, "You never said anything about being a school teacher." He was grateful she was in his arms, but wished they were alone. He couldn't stop thinking about the kiss they'd shared that afternoon, about the feel of her body stretched on top of his while he made love to her sweet mouth.

"It seems funny to say it never came up, but it didn't. Everything has happened so fast." So very fast, like the way her heart was beating just being in his arms. "I keep telling myself we only met yesterday, but it doesn't feel that way. It's the same with your friends. Within minutes of meeting them, I felt like I'd known them for years. They're wonderful, Logan. And this has been…well, just about the best night of my life."

"Yeah. You're aces with them, too."

Paige racked her brain for topics of conversation. She was afraid if she didn't talk about ordinary, mundane…anything, she'd say what was really on her mind. Like how much she loved being in his arms. Like how much she wanted to kiss him. "Uh, speaking of jobs, I just realized I don't know what you do for a living."

"Research." As far as euphemisms went it was okay. He didn't want to lie to Paige, but after the way she'd reacted to finding out he was an ex-cop he wasn't ready for her to know he was a private investigator. In fact, he'd confided to Cade and Reese his theory that she was running from something or somebody and cautioned them to avoid any mention of his job. Thank goodness Cade had diverted attention from Belle's comment.

"Medical? Scientific?"

"Sorry, Red. Nothing so grand as all that. We collect data for our clients. Background checks, that sort of thing."

"You mean like when you apply for a job and the personnel department checks your résumé?"

"Yeah." he said, relieved she had jumped to a logical, if not wholly accurate conclusion.

"You said, 'we.'"

"My partner, Rick Conner, is handling the business. That's how I'm able to take this time off."

"The man who called yesterday?"

"Yeah." He'd completely forgotten to return Rick's call. This thing with Paige was occupying all his thoughts.

"Oh." And with that brilliant response her supply of chitchat had ended, and thankfully, so had the song. She didn't wait for the next one, but headed back to the table, leaving Logan to follow. Reese and Shea weren't far behind and they all got to the table about the same time.

"Well," Shea said, putting a hand to her lower back. "Time for another potty run. Excuse me, everyone." After a kiss from Reese, she waddled off.

"I'm gonna have another beer," Reese announced. "Logan?"

"Sure."

"How about you, Cade?"

"Nope. Time for Chance to hit the hay."

"Way past," Belle concurred. "I'll bet Posey has a bottle warmed and waiting."

"Y'all just keep on relaxin'," Cade said. "We'll be back directly."

Reese and Logan headed toward a galvanized washtub containing the iced-down long-necks the three men favored.

Cade scooped the baby out of his high chair and into his arms, and the three of them started across the patio. Just as they reached the stairs leading to the house, the soft strains of George Strait's "You Look So Good In Love" drifted from the stereo. Cade stopped, reached for his wife and pulled her into his arms. He kissed her, then, still holding Chance, and he and Belle began to dance.

Paige was absolutely enthralled with the picture they presented, doting parents and child, heads almost touching as they swayed to the music. She watched as Cade and Belle kissed their son, then each other. Clearly, the portrait of a loving family. But, it was the look that passed between husband and wife that made Paige catch her breath. Never in her life had she witnessed so much conveyed in a glance. It was love, respect, desire, worship, trust and a thousand other things she couldn't begin to describe all rolled up into a single, lingering, stunningly unforgettable look. Instinctively, she dug into her purse for a pencil, then glanced around, searching for paper she could use. Desperate for anything to work with, she tore off an entire corner of the heavy-gauge paper tablecloth covering the picnic table and started to sketch.

Knowing the song wouldn't last long, her hand moved as if possessed. She'd never worked so fast before, but she *had* to capture the magic happening right before her eyes. The tilt of Belle's head as she gazed into Cade's eyes. The way he held them all together as they moved to the music. Little Chance's gurgling smile. She was so focused, so intent on what she was doing she didn't even notice Shea had returned and was standing behind her, watching her work. But even if she had realized it, she couldn't have looked up, couldn't risk losing even one second. What she saw was simply too precious and rare.

Then the song ended, and so did the dance, and the three continued up the steps and into the house. Then and only then, did Paige stop. She sighed, the moment gone, and let the pencil drop to the table.

"Paige," Shea said, softly.

"Oh." Paige glanced up. "I'm sorry. I didn't realized you'd come back."

"No, you were…transfixed is the best word I

can think of. I've never seen anything like it. Or that.'' She pointed to the drawing.

''Oh, it's just a sketch.'' She started to wad the paper up in her hand.

''No! Don't!'' Shea put her hand on Paige's to prevent her from wrinkling it further. Her demand drew the attention of Reese and Logan and they strolled back to the table.

''What's going on over here?''

''Paige did a sketch of Cade, Belle and the baby, and she was about to throw it away when I stopped her.'' Shea looked directly at Paige. ''I didn't mean to shout, but I just couldn't let you destroy something so…exceptional.''

''That's nice of you, but it's not very good. And I can't believe I was so rude as to tear Belle's tablecloth.''

''Reese, Logan, you've got to see this.'' Very carefully, Shea smoothed the paper flat on the table, then moved the decorative hurricane lantern closer and motioned for them to take a look.

Reese was the first to comment. After staring at the drawing for a moment, he bent down, balancing himself on the balls of his feet. It brought him closer to the picture and Paige. ''You have a gift,'' he said, looking right into her eyes.

''He's right,'' Shea said, her voice filled with awe. ''There's so much depth and texture, if you touched the drawing you'd expect to feel the warmth of their skin.''

''Please,'' Paige protested, unaccustomed to having her work receive such praise. ''It's not that big a deal. If I'd had my sketch pad I could have done a much better job.''

"A better job of what?" Cade asked, as he and Belle rejoined them.

Reese, Shea and Logan made room for two of the artist's subjects. Belle looked down at the sketch and her hands flew to her mouth. "Oh, oh, gracious. It's—it's..." Her gaze went to Paige. "You did this?"

"Y-yes." She couldn't tell if what she saw in Belle's eyes was shock or pleasure.

"It's...wonderful. No. Wonderful is too pale a word for what you've created."

"Oh, thank you," she said, relieved. "But I didn't create it. You did. I just put down on paper what I saw."

"You've done more than that," Cade added. Then glancing at Belle for agreement, he asked, "Would you mind if we kept the sketch?"

Stunned, Paige stared at them. When she didn't answer, Belle and Cade exchanged looks of confusion. "I know artists are attached to their work, but we'd be happy to pay whatever—"

"Oh, no. No, I couldn't take money. It's just..." She couldn't believe they actually thought it was good enough to keep. "It's on a torn paper tablecloth," she repeated as if that declared it's worthlessness.

"We don't care," they said in unison and everyone laughed.

Paige couldn't help but smile. "At least let me redo it when I get a good sketch pad and pencils."

"Great. Wonderful," Belle said. "But I'd still like to have this one, if that's all right."

Paige picked up the sketch and handed it to

her. "I'm honored." And she was. More than she could express.

Everybody seemed to take a deep breath and smile at once. All except one. Standing beside Reese, Logan had looked at her work for a long time, but hadn't made one single comment. She couldn't tell by looking at his eyes if that was good or bad. And she realized that as much as she had enjoyed the compliments she'd received tonight, she was waiting for Logan's opinion. It shouldn't make any difference. But it did.

Shea yawned sleepily before she caught herself. "Sorry." She grinned. "I just can't seem to get enough sleep these days."

"Too bad you can't save it up for when you need it. Like for 3 a.m. feedings," Belle said.

"On that note," Reese helped Shea to her feet, "I think we'll head for home."

The departure of the Barretts signaled the end of the evening and soon Logan and Paige were headed back into Sweetwater Springs. As he guided the motorcycle down the highway, Logan thought about what a surprise his damsel in distress had turned out to be.

First, an artist. He couldn't get the image of her drawing out of his mind. He was no art lover and certainly not a critic, but he didn't need a Ph.D. in Art Appreciation to recognize that Paige had talent. Real talent. No, a gift. That's what Reese had called it, and he was right. She'd not only captured physical characteristics perfectly, but she'd captured the spirits of her subjects and a depth of emotion that was staggering. There was strength and power, tenderness and beauty in her work. And that same strength and power, tenderness and beauty was the heart of Paige. Whether she realized it or not, and he doubted she did, her work held a mirror to her emotions, even her soul.

And a teacher. She'd taught children and even wanted to open an art school for underprivileged kids.

But the biggest surprise had come at the beginning of the evening when she hadn't sidestepped the fact of their kiss. She'd addressed it head-on. He was beginning to realize that Paige wasn't the frivolous piece of fluff he'd taken her for at first. He'd known she had style from the minute he'd laid eyes on her. Tonight he saw the substance.

Try as she might, Paige couldn't understand why Logan hadn't made one single comment about her sketch, unless he didn't like it at all. Until that moment, she hadn't realized how important his opinion was. By the time they reached the farmhouse, she decided he wasn't going to comment, so she started upstairs to bed.

"Paige."

Her hand on the newel post, she turned to face him. "Yes?"

"Thanks."

"For what?"

He shrugged. "For coming with me. For such a good time."

"Believe me, the pleasure was all mine. I should be thanking you. And I do."

"You're welcome."

They stared at each for several seconds. Finally, Logan grinned. "Well, I'll say this for us. We're polite, if nothing else."

Paige smiled back. "Your grandmother would be proud."

"Guess she would at that."

She started to say good-night, but hesitated. No, she wasn't going to sleep until she found out what she wanted to know. "Logan, I don't want to sound vain, but did you not like my sketch? I mean, if you didn't, it's fine. Or maybe you—"

"It was…" He took a deep breath and so did she, waiting. "…just about the most beautiful thing I'd ever seen."

She smiled, instantly. "Really?"

Until that moment Logan had never truly seen anyone's face light up. Hers did, green eyes sparkling, cheeks glowing. No, he thought, she was just about the most beautiful thing he'd ever seen. "Yeah," he said, smiling back at her. "It knocked my socks off."

Paige's pent-up breath escaped her in a whoosh. "Thanks."

He crossed to where she stood, resting his hand on the banister inches from hers. "Believe me, the pleasure was all mine," he quoted her words back to her.

Paige glanced at their hands so close they were almost touching and for half a second she thought—hoped—he was going to kiss her. But seconds passed and the moment slipped away. "Well," she said. "Guess I'll see you in the morning."

"Guess so."

"Good night."

"'Night, Rusty." As he watched her climb the stairs he wanted to kick himself for not kissing her. The only thing that held him back was that he was afraid once he started he wouldn't be able to stop.

COFFEE WAS BREWING and the back door was open when Paige came downstairs to fix breakfast bright and early the next morning. Through the screen door she could see Logan bent over a lawn mower, a wrench in his hand. He was wearing jeans, old ones faded nearly to white at the seams. The soft, supple denim molded to the muscles in his legs like a glove. His shirt was old denim as well, equally faded, and the sleeves had been ripped off at the seams, exposing his well-developed arms. And he hadn't bothered to button it, which bothered her a lot, in a way that had nothing to do with proper dress. He was just so…male, he made her mouth water.

"Goo—" She cleared her throat. "Good morning."

He glanced up, smiling that lazy smile that had her heart beat jumping. "Morning, Rusty. You sleep all right?"

The question was delivered at the same pace as his smile, but now she knew his slow-walking, slow-talking style was deceptive. There was nothing slow or lazy about him. Certainly not when he kissed her. "Fine. I slept…fine."

"Glad to hear it." He slipped a hand inside the unbuttoned shirt and patted his flat, hard-muscled stomach. "You got a hungry man on your hands. How 'bout some pancakes?"

"Pancakes?" She licked her lips. "Uh, sure," she said, hoping there was a box of mix in the pantry so she didn't have to start from scratch. "How many?"

He looked straight into her eyes. "Like I said, you got a man with a powerful hunger on your hands. I'll take whatever you'll give me."

Paige couldn't get her breath and she felt light-headed. Was he still talking about pancakes?

"But say, a half dozen to begin with?"

She nodded, then found her way to the pantry. Once there, she leaned against the door facing and took several deep breaths. Merciful heaven! The man was potent. A few more seconds of deep breathing and she felt steady enough to handle a frying pan and a griddle.

Thankfully, there was a box of mix in the pantry and soon she was whipping up batter while bacon sizzled in a pan on the stove. The first fat circle of mixture was on the griddle when she heard the screen door slam. She glanced over her shoulder to see Logan walking straight to her. He stopped directly behind her. Then he leaned forward, reaching for a cup hanging on a rack mounted to the side of one of the cabinets, and his shirt gapped open. He was so close she felt the heat from his body, so close her elbow was only inches from that hard-muscled stomach she'd admired minutes ago.

He sniffed the air, his eyes on her. "Love the smell of bacon frying, don't you?"

"Uh," she said, stupidly, his nearness, his maleness driving logical thought from her brain.

If she leaned just the tiniest bit closer, their lips would be close enough to—

"Careful."

"What?"

"You'll burn the bacon," he said, slowly lifting the cup from the hook.

"Oh." She turned back to her work. Reluctantly.

"Give a yell when they're ready," he said, not moving away.

"O-okay." She flipped the fluffy pancake and was amazed it didn't wind up on the ceiling, her hands were trembling so much. When he did step away, it was as if someone had turned off a heater. A second later the screen door slammed. Paige slumped against the stove, wondering if she'd even have enough strength left to take that wild walk she wanted.

Ten minutes later she set a huge stack of pancakes, a plate of bacon and a tall glass of orange juice in front of Logan and watched him devour his breakfast while she nibbled at hers. Her appetite, for food anyway, had waned. But her appetite for watching him only increased. Her artist's eye focused on his hands, wide and strong. Even so simple a task as using a knife and fork fascinated her. While he ate, she noted his jaw, straight lines, well defined. And his mouth... She could watch his mouth for hours, maybe days. Like everything else about him, it was strong. But she knew it was also a seductive mouth. A pleasure-giving mouth.

Logan watched her watching him, so intent she didn't even realize her lips were parted so invitingly. She was mentally sketching him, he decided, and the thought pleased him. That meant she was thinking about him, focusing on him and not with any ideas of moonlight and roses. She would concentrate on the physical. His eyes, and the way they looked at her. His mouth, and the way he kissed her. His hands, and the way he'd held her; maybe the way they could stroke her, caress her. Suddenly, he laid his fork down and pushed his plate away, not sure just whose concentration was more intent, hers or his.

"You want more?" she asked, innocently.

"No. Think I've had just about all I can handle for right now." He wiped his mouth with a paper napkin and forced himself to think nonsexual thoughts. "Say, how would you like to take in a rodeo?"

"A rodeo? In Sweetwater Springs?"

"Kinda. Cade mentioned that several of the local ranchers get together a couple of times a year and put on a small one. The ranchers all kick in a little prize money, but it's not PRCA sanctioned or anything. Just a bunch of cowhands gettin' together. They pick a spot, then everybody just sort of passes the word for a 'y'all come' rodeo."

"PRCA?"

"Professional Rodeo Cowboys' Association. All the rodeos on the official circuit have to be PRCA sanctioned for the cowboys to earn points."

Suddenly she remembered him introducing his friends as "broke-down old bull riders." "Cade and Reese were in the rodeo, weren't they?"

"Yeah."

"You, too?"

He nodded. "They were bull riders. I did calf ropin' competitions for a couple of years."

"Why did you quit?"

"As best as I recall, I gave it up when I figured out the dollar-to-bone ratio."

"I don't understand."

"Well, all three of us had a real good day at the Mesquite Rodeo. Had a little prize money in our pockets, feeling fine and hell-bent on drinking the town dry. After some, no, a lot of beer we sat down and figured out how many bones we'd broken compared to how much money we'd made. Fortunately, when I sobered up I remembered the figures and decided there had to be a better way to earn a living."

Paige laughed. "I take it the ratio was not good."

"Not worth a damn. You'd think after that I'd have picked a calmer profession, but I went from ropin' calves to ropin' criminals."

"Oh. Yes, I—I remember you mentioned being a police officer."

"Now, that sure enough made my grandmother happy."

"But it's so dangerous."

"Guess it's in the genes. My grandfather was a Texas Ranger and his father was a U.S. Marshall. Mimi didn't like the danger, but she was proud of my work. So was I, for a while."

"What happened? I'm sorry," she rushed to apologize. "That was terribly rude, and it's none of my business."

"It's okay. My partner was killed by a drug dealer—"

"Oh, Logan." She put her hand on his arm. "How awful for you."

"Yeah," he said, moved by the warmth of her touch, her compassion. "Sam was a good guy. We used to complain about what a revolving door the criminal justice system had become, but neither of us ever figured we'd get tangled up in it. I caught the guy that shot Sam, he went to trial…and got off on a technicality. All legal, mind you. But that did it for me. I loved being a cop, but after that my heart wasn't in it. And when that happens, you might as well get out because sooner or later either you'll get somebody killed or wind up dead yourself."

After a long silence, Logan covered her hand with his. "Sorry. That's probably more information than you wanted."

"No, I'm glad you told me. It makes me feel…" She almost said, closer to you, but changed her mind. "…like I know you better. And I'm glad you asked me to see a rodeo."

"On second thought," Logan said. "The rodeo is tomorrow afternoon."

"So?"

"Isn't your friend supposed to show up in Paris soon?" The not-so-subtle reminder was a dirty trick, but he wanted to see how she would react.

"Oh…yes. But I told you Regi is unpredictable." She toyed with the handle of her coffee cup. "Would you mind…uh, would it upset your plans if I had to stay awhile longer?"

Logan grinned. "Not even a little bit." His plans were based on her staying, at least long enough for them to share a couple of wild nights of loving.

"Then, if I'm still here, I'd love to see the rodeo with you," she said, knowing full well she had already made the decision *not* to call Regi. Knowing she had already decided to become Logan Walker's lover.

7

PAIGE HAD GONE over it in her head a hundred times, but no matter which justification she tried or how she couched her words, the results were the same. Basically, she was planning to tell a bald-faced lie. The only question left for her to answer was when. Did she tell him tonight, or wait until tomorrow? He was showering at the moment, so she could pretend she'd called Regi…no, she couldn't say she called now. There was a seven-hour time difference, so she would have to wait until tomorrow. Damn. She wished it was done, over. This lying business was hard on the nerves. So, she would tell her lie tomorrow. Early so she wouldn't have to fret over it for hours.

Then, of course, all she had to do was tell Logan she wanted to have sex with him.

A knock on the door interrupted her train of thought and she looked up to see the pizza delivery boy standing at the door. Paige paid for the pizza with a twenty-dollar bill Logan had left on the kitchen counter, then put the delivery box on the table. She walked to the bottom of the stairs, calling up to him, "Pizza's here." A couple of seconds later, Logan came down the stairs. He hadn't bothered with a shirt, or shoes. Drying his still damp hair with a towel, he was only wearing a pair of jeans. Another pair like the ones he'd worn that morning, faded but a superb fit. Except they were zipped but not...

Snapped.

As he took each stair—and he was in no hurry, as usual—his hips moved, causing the unsnapped waistband to flap ever so slightly, the brass snap catching the light. Absurdly, Paige thought it was winking at her. "Forgot you washed all my T-shirts this afternoon," he said, letting the towel slide down his head to hang around his neck. "I'll get one out of the laundry basket and be with you in a sec."

Paige stood with her mouth open watching him walk away from her, the smooth muscles of his back and shoulders a graceful play of power. She had never been a purveyor of men's butts, but that could change, starting now. Trim and taut, his was spectacular. "Uh, what? Oh, yeah, sure."

Logan smiled to himself. He was no Arnold Schwarzenegger, but he knew he had a better-than-average body, especially his shoulders and back. More than one woman had commented favorably on both. He wasn't above maximizing his good points in order to impress Paige. And from the look on her face, he'd say he'd scored a couple of points. He figured leaving his jeans unsnapped was good for at least five more. Grabbing a T-shirt, he tossed the damp towel on top of the washing machine. He had one item left in his little bag of tricks.

"Let's take the pizza into the parlor and see

what's on the tube," he suggested, making no move to carry the box.

"Okay. That sounds—"

Logan grabbed the hem of the T-shirt in both hands and pulled it over his head, taking his time stretching the soft cotton fabric down over his broad shoulders. Then he unzipped his jeans—and thought he heard her breath catch—tucked in his shirt, then zipped and snapped them. All accomplished very naturally. All done at an unhurried, but not necessarily slow, pace.

"All set," he announced, innocently. Still shoeless, he walked to the refrigerator. "I'm gonna have a beer. How about you?"

"C-cola."

He pulled out a Lone Star long-neck beer and a Coke. "You got it." Drinks in one hand, he picked up the pizza box and walked into the parlor.

Paige took a deep shuddering breath and followed him. He set the pizza on the coffee table, then sat down on the floor, giving her the sofa.

"Want to see if there's a decent movie on?" he asked, after practically inhaling his first slice of pizza.

"Sure."

After ten minutes of flipping through channels of infomercials, black-and-white WWII movies and reruns, they gave up, switched off the TV and tuned in a local country radio station.

"Mercy," Paige said, after finishing her fourth slice of pizza. "I never eat like that."

Logan put down his sixth slice and pivoted on his fanny so he'd be facing her. "You burned a lot of calories today; got to restock. You washed the curtains in the kitchen, dining room and in here. Washed clothes. Cooked two meals. Made lemonade for me while I mowed the lawn. Polished furniture.'' He raised his half-empty long-neck in salute. ''You worked your butt off and did a damned fine job.''

''Thanks.'' Glancing around the parlor at the way the furniture gleamed, unblemished by a speck of dust, Paige smiled, proud of herself. It did look nice, if she said so herself. ''I like this house. It's...''

''Old. And needs a lot of work.''

''No, it's not. I mean it is, but that's its charm. It's the only house I've been in that really feels like a home. People lived and laughed in these rooms.''

''My grandmother loved it so much she wouldn't leave. When she got sick and had to have someone to look after her, she refused to go to a nursing home, so we hired a live-in nurse. At that, she still got up before sunrise to feed the chickens, just like she had for over sixty years.'' A sadness filled his eyes. ''Until she couldn't get out of bed anymore.''

''What happened to the chickens?''

''Sold 'em.''

Something in his voice told her that unenviable task had fallen to him. ''You loved her a lot, didn't you?''

''She raised me. My mother died when I was about seven. My dad didn't handle it very well, and he had the ranch and a business to run, a feedlot.'' His voice drifted off and she could see that he was lost in a memory. "Somebody had to wipe my nose when it was runny and blister my butt when it was needed. And believe me, it needed it a lot. Anyway, Mimi took on the job and never batted an eye."

"Where was your grandfather?"

"He died in a ranching accident when I was just a toddler."

"Any brothers and sisters?"

"Nope."

"Me either. Are you close to your father?"

"That's a hard question. When I was growing up I thought he was kind of distant, set in his ways and he was always working. We never talked much. Then he remarried a couple of years ago." Logan arched an eyebrow. "A younger woman. And I can tell you it didn't set too well with me at first, but now…"

"Now?"

He grinned. "Hell, they travel all over the world. Dad's learned to scuba dive, snow ski."

"That's wonderful."

"Yeah." He took a long swig of beer. "I don't see a whole lot of him, but he's happy. That's all I care about." He took another drink. "So what about you? Your family."

"There's really not much to tell."

When she didn't elaborate, which he expected, he prodded her. "Aw, c'mon, Rusty. There's gotta be something to tell. Are they moonshiners, ax murderers, or what?"

"Ax murderers. I was hoping you wouldn't find out, but you guessed it."

"So is Borden a family name on your mother's side or your old man's?"

They laughed and, for the first time since walking in on Randal the Rat, Paige didn't feel the wave of animosity sweep over her whenever she thought of her family.

"My dad works too hard and my mother…well, she pretty much runs the family." Paige glanced around the parlor again. "You know, it's funny. I grew up with my grandmother living in the same house with us, but I don't have real warm memories of her the way you do of Mimi."

"Some families are just naturally closer than others."

"No, I don't think it's natural. It's something you have to work at." She looked down at her hands and sighed. "My parents didn't work at it very hard."

"Were they strict?"

"My mother was…is." She looked up. "What about your grandmother?"

"Oh yeah." Logan grinned. "When Mimi laid down the law you knew you better walk the straight and narrow. And she didn't care how many birthdays I had or how tall I grew. Worst punishment I ever got was when I was sixteen."

"I'll bet a girl was involved."

"Now, what makes you say that?"

"Because I'll bet you, Cade, Reese and…" She tried to remember the name of the fourth in the Fearsome Foursome.

"Sloan?"

"Yes. I'll bet you were all hellraisers *and* heart-breakers."

"I don't kiss and tell." He gave her his best aw-shucks grin. "But this time you're half right. I had Sunday dinner with this girl I was sweet on. In my defense, I had good intentions of going back into the house and thank her mom for the meal, but…I got distracted and forgot."

"Let me guess. The distraction was the girl."

Still grinning, he shook his head. "Package deal. The girl and the kiss."

"Ahh."

"See, with Mimi it was manners by ear."

"By ear?"

"Yeah. If I didn't mind my manners she grabbed me by the ear and hauled me off for a good talkin' to. And I sure as hell got one that day. The girl's mother called and just happened to mention she didn't know if I liked the meal, 'cause I never thanked her. Don't tell me some big old broad-shouldered football player never made you forget your manners?"

Paige laughed. "Not like that."

"C'mon. I'll bet the boys buzzed around you like bees to a honeycomb."

"Not really. I didn't have a steady boyfriend until after college."

"What happened to him?"

"I left him when I found him in bed with one of my best friends."

"Get a rope," Logan said seriously even though he was smiling. "Any man that dumb deserves to be hung." Then the smile faded. "So he broke your heart, huh?"

"As a matter of fact, no. It was a good thing that I found out he was cheating on me or I never would have realized I didn't love him. We'd known each other most of our lives. Our parents were close friends. Everybody expected us to be together and we just went along with it."

"Bet your folks were upset when you called it off."

"Not in the way you might think," she said with a derisive laugh. "My mother urged me to think over walking out for the sake of the family name. The scandal, you know." Suddenly, Paige stretched her long legs the length of the sofa. "You know you forgot to add something to my list of accomplishments today."

"How's that?" He knew a change of subject when he heard one and figured she decided she had said too much.

"You forgot to add shopping spree. I can't thank you enough for buying me a sketch pad and pencils."

"Gotta have the right tools to do the job."

"Just the same, I appreciate it very much. And for these." She ran her hands down her denim-clad legs. "They're the most comfortable, best-fitting pair of jeans I've ever owned."

"They ought to be. You bought 'em already broke in."

"But that's fashionable. Everybody does…" She had been about to say everybody does it these days, referring to her trendy circle of friends. "I can't believe I got these for only four dollars at that resale shop. You'd be stunned to know what some people are willing to pay for 'already broke in.'" She looked up in time to see his gaze move down her body then back up to her face.

"All I know is that you look great in 'em." His voice dropped to that low, sexy drawl that never failed to turn her knees to butter and her will-power to water.

Just that quick, the room became still, quiet…and intimate. Just that quick, her heartbeat jumped and heat flashed from the top of her head right down to the Spicy Apricot Frost polish on her toenails. Just that quick, his intense blue eyes darkened with passion.

"Do I?" she asked.

"They show off your long sexy legs."

"I didn't…I didn't think you'd ever notice."

"Yeah. I noticed." He stared at her mouth for seconds that ticked by like hours, then his gaze went to the pulse beat at the base of her throat. When he finally lifted his gaze to hers, he saw desire in her green eyes. Desire and willingness.

Logan knew if he stayed where he was he'd kiss her. And if he kissed her, they'd both be naked in a matter of minutes. He didn't consider that a brag. Not the way she was looking at him so needy, so…hot. Here was his chance for a night of wild loving. His golden opportunity.

And he wasn't going to take it.

The realization stunned him. Why on God's green earth was he backing off from something he wanted so badly? It wasn't fear of rejection. All he had to do was look into her eyes to see she was at least on the same wavelength, if not even more than willing. It wasn't fear they might get carried away and forget protection. The foil-wrapped condom in his jeans pocket covered that. Then what the hell was holding him back?

Fear of her leaving. Fear that if he made love to her tonight, and she left tomorrow, he would feel worse than if he'd never touched her. Insane as it sounded he knew it was true. Something...that spark of hunger he couldn't quite identify kept him from reaching for her now. It all went back to the lust versus longing he'd felt when they first met. He felt that same tug-of-war tonight and he didn't understand it any better now than he had then.

Lust he could handle. But he still wasn't sure about the longing.

He sat watching her, knowing she was waiting for him to make his move. Knowing the decision was his. Slowly, carefully, he downed the last of his beer and got to his feet.

"It's been a long day." He offered her his hand to help her up and she took it. "I don't know about you, but all of a sudden I'm dragging."

She stared at him for a minute as if she intended to say something, then changed her mind. "Yes," she said, finally. "It has been a long day."

He stretched lazily. "Why don't you go on and I'll lock up?"

"All right."

"Rusty," he said when she reached the bottom of the stairs.

"Yes?"

"It was a real nice evening. I enjoyed talking."

"Yes, it was nice. Well...good night."

"'Night."

Logan watched until she turned the corner of the landing and disappeared from sight. Poor baby. She was confused. And she had a right to be. In her shoes, he'd probably be mad as an ornery bull. He couldn't even hazard a guess about her experience, and for that matter didn't want to, but he didn't figure her for a shy virgin. She knew what was on his mind tonight. She'd sent him enough signals and he'd all but said thanks, but no thanks. No wonder she was confused. Logan just hoped he had a chance to make it up to her. And he sure as hell hoped tomorrow brought him another go round at that golden opportunity.

But that wasn't his only problem. As time went on, he struggled more and more with the fact that she would probably run if she knew he was a P.I. But there just never seemed to be a right time to tell her. That reminded him that he hadn't returned Rick's call and he went downstairs. A moment or two later, he hung up after leaving a message for Rick. Things were getting complicated.

PAIGE CLOSED THE door to her room, leaning against it for a moment. She'd been so sure Logan wanted to kiss her, or more, yet he hadn't. He had to have known she wouldn't refuse him. She'd all but told him she'd been waiting for him to notice her that way. Then she remembered something he'd said the first day they met. That if a woman wanted him all she had to do was say so. Maybe that's what it would take. Maybe she would have to be so direct he couldn't misunderstand.

Of course, there was always the chance he would refuse.

Not make love to Logan. Never? She shivered and wrapped her arms around herself. The thought made her cold in a way that had nothing to do with temperature. Cold all the way to her heart. Suddenly, what had begun as another aspect of her new life had turned into something unexpected. Something that felt so good and so frightening she was afraid to put a name to it. Could she have fallen for Logan? No, that wasn't possible. Was it? After all, she'd only known him a few days.

But how long did it take to fall in love?

Could it happen in the time it takes to say hello? Or glance across a crowded room? Or maybe, possibly, the length of a kiss?

What had seemed a simple decision yesterday wasn't so simple anymore. She still wanted Logan. Desperately. She still wanted to make love with him, but her reasons were greater, deeper than she'd realized. As great and deep as her love for him. Maybe her heart had followed its instincts and led her where she needed to be. Fate, she decided, was a curious thing indeed.

LOGAN STARTED PAINTING the outside of the house before sunup the next day and worked without stopping until after noon. Paige had already finished her sandwich when she heard him washing up in the breezeway. He came through the back door, walked straight to the pitcher of iced tea Paige had made, poured himself a tall tumbler full and downed it in one long drink.

"I, uh, called Paris," Paige said.

Slowly, Logan lowered the tumbler. "Get in touch with your friend?"

"Yes…"

Everything inside him went very still. Dead still.

"And no. I didn't actually speak with her, but she, uh, she canceled her reservation and the clerk said he gave her my message."

"And?"

"Nothing. She got the message late yesterday afternoon and she hasn't called."

"So, what does that mean?"

"It means Regi is off being Regi. Sooner or later she'll remember that I called, but that could be tonight or next week. It means I…I need to stay."

Until that moment Logan hadn't realized how much he wanted to hear that answer. How much he wanted her to stay. He sat the empty glass on the counter and looked at her. "Well, then it looks like you and I are going to a rodeo."

Paige smiled brightly. "It sure does."

"Well, don't just stand there, Red. Get your rear in gear."

She turned and hurried upstairs to shower and change. "And leave me some hot water," he called after her. Grinning from ear to ear, he poured himself another glass of iced tea then bit into one of two BLTs she had fixed for him.

Damn, he felt good.

Forty-five minutes later he was still feeling good as he locked the back door to the farmhouse and walked to the bike where Paige stood putting on her helmet.

"How far is it to this arena?"

"Not far from Cade and Belle's place. It belongs to a rancher by the name of Case O'Brian."

"Will there be a lot of spectators? I mean, considering this isn't...what did you call it?"

"PRCA sanctioned."

"Yes."

"Darlin', around here if it's got a bull, a calf and just two cowboys with only one rope between 'em, it draws a crowd. Doesn't take much to entertain folks in these parts."

Paige understood what he meant when she got her first glimpse of the small arena surrounded by pickup trucks and horse trailers. Two sections of bleachers were set up on one side of the arena and they were full. It did appear that a lot of people liked rodeos, even the "y'all come" variety.

Because the earth around the arena was slightly soft, Logan opted to leave the Harley at the end of the hard-packed dirt road leading up to the area. Once they were off the bike, he opened the trunk and removed two Stetsons. He handed one to her.

"What's this for?"

"To keep that cute little nose of yours from getting sunburned."

"Oh, good, thanks." She put the hat on, positioning it on the back of her head.

Logan took one look at the hat and shook his

head. "Well, that's going to do a whole hell of a lot of good. Bring it forward, like this," he instructed, settling his own hat low on his forehead so that the brim shaded his beautiful blue eyes. "See?"

Paige blinked, astonished at the transformation wrought by the Stetson. In a split second he'd gone from easy rider to roping the wind. Once she'd had difficulty imaging him on a horse with a rope in his hands, but looking at him now, she couldn't think why. It was just jeans, boots, a white long-sleeve Western-cut shirt and the hat, that's all. No, that wasn't all. It was the man. He just simply took her breath away.

"Here, let me." He brushed a wave of rusty red curls away from her face before situating her hat. "There."

"How do I look?" she asked, unable to take her eyes off his handsome face. She recognized the intensity of his gaze for what it was. Heat. Power. She welcomed all of it.

He took a step toward her. "You look good enough to—"

"Logan Walker." A tall, dark-haired man, a touch of gray at his temples, slapped Logan on the back. "Long time no see. Where you been keepin' yourself?"

Reluctantly, Logan directed his gaze away from Paige to the newcomer. "Case, how've you been?"

"Fine, fine."

"Paige O'Neil, this is our host, Case—"

"O'Brian. Pleased to meetcha, ma'am." He

shook her hand then turned to Logan. "Well, now I see what's been keeping you busy. 'Course, what a woman this good-looking sees in your worthless hide is beyond me."

"Speaking of worthless hides, how's Dev?"

"Off on one of his snapshot safaris. I'm beginning to think he'll never settle down. Oh, I almost forgot. Here you go." And he handed Logan a white square with a black number printed on it. "Good luck," he said. Then he tipped his hat to Paige, "Ms. O'Neil," and moved on to hand out more numbers.

Suddenly, she realized those were contestant numbers. "Logan, you're not—"

"Not what?"

"Going to compete." She gestured toward the cluster of cowboys with similar numbers on their backs hanging off some of the rails or waiting for their turn at the current event.

"You bet."

"But, you ride a motorcycle for goodness sake. You're not a regular…"

"Working cowboy? No, but I've kept my hand in. Cade usually cons me into working a few days whenever I visit. Besides, it's just for fun."

"But you might get hurt if you haven't done this in a while."

"Not to worry." Logan smiled. "Rodeoin's like a religion, darlin'. No matter how far you stray, you don't ever completely lose your faith."

"But—"

"I see Belle and Shea over in the stands. Why don't you join them?"

She turned to look for them. "All right, but—"

When she turned back, Logan was walking toward the cluster of cowboys. "Damn you, Logan," she whispered. "Don't you dare go and get yourself hurt."

Resigned that there was no way to stop him, she scanned the grandstands for Belle and Shea. "Hi," she said when she reached them a few minutes later.

"Couldn't talk Logan out of competing, huh?" Belle said.

"No."

"Neither could we." Shea pointed to where Cade and Reese stood near the chutes.

"Your husbands at least do this kind of work on a regular basis. I'm worried Logan will get hurt."

Shea and Belle looked at each other, then at Paige. "Join the club," they said together.

"This is only my second time," Shea said, "and fourth for Belle."

"We sit up here cheering them on, pretending everything is peachy, and all the time our hearts are in our throats. Of course, I'd never tell Cade that," Belle added.

The three women spent the next hour taking turns worrying as each of their men either competed or worked as arena riders helping the other contestants. Reese was the first to compete. While Shea explained the finer points of the event, they waited. Then suddenly steer and cowboy were tearing across the arena, and before Paige realized it, Reese had roped the steer, dismounted, tied the steer off and both his hands shot into the air, signaling he was done.

When it came time for Logan to participate in team calf roping she held her breath, grateful, at least, that he wasn't in the bull riding or bulldogging events. Again the signal was given, only this time the steer and two men dashed the length of the arena. Logan's rope lashed out, catching the horns while the other cowboy's rope snagged the back hooves. It all happened so fast and looked so easy, but Paige knew from what Belle and Shea had told her that it was neither. All the events, even the ones that went smoothly, were dangerous, especially the bull riding, which was the last event of the day.

As the afternoon wore on, the temperature climbed and Paige was thankful for her hat. Poor Shea had a hat, too, but it didn't do much to shade her rounded belly.

"I'm not sure how much longer I'm going to last," she said, pulling a small battery-operated fan from her purse and training the fan's breeze on her face and neck.

"Would you like for me to get you something to drink?" Paige asked.

"I think my husband has beaten you to it."

"Would you look at that?" Belle said, watching Cade, Reese and Logan walk toward the catering wagon set up to serve barbeque, cold beer and soft drinks. "Have you ever seen three better-looking men in your life?"

"Nope." Shea sighed. "A triple threat if ever I saw one."

"I'll bet every female out here has given them the eye."

"But two of them are married," Paige said.

"Damn straight," Belle quoted one of her husband's favorite comments. "That doesn't keep the ladies from looking. And wishing."

It was true. They were three gorgeous male specimens. And Paige was suddenly overcome with pride knowing that she would be going home with one of them.

Belle nudged Paige as the three men started up the bleacher steps with refreshments. "Just watch the heads turn and the eyelashes flutter."

"Where are they?" Frowning, Shea scanned the spectators. "I'll scratch their eyes out."

Then all three laughed at the absurdity of the remark, considering Shea's advanced pregnancy and lack of mobility.

"And if you think this is bad, wait until the reunion dance tomorrow night. You're going, aren't you?" Belle asked. "Logan told us you weren't leaving town right away."

Paige shrugged. "He hasn't asked me. And even if he did, I don't have clothes to wear to a dance."

"Of course he'll ask you," Belle assured her. "As for clothes, the information from the reunion committee said casual attire. There will be people there in everything from jeans to sequins."

"Too bad you're taller than I am," Shea put in. "I've got a whole closetful of clothes I can't wear."

"You're more than welcome to borrow something of mine," Belle added.

"I..." Paige looked from one to the other, overwhelmed by their generosity. "Thank you. You've both been so kind to me."

"Oh, phoo," Shea said. "We like you and you're fun."

"Y'all having a good time?" Cade asked as the men joined them a moment later, bringing cold bottled water.

"I've had all the good time I can stand." Shea took one of the bottles and held it to her cheek. Looking at her husband, she patted her stomach. "Take us home, cowboy. It's too hot, and I'm too fat."

Reese glanced at Cade. "Sorry I won't be here to see you land in the dirt, but duty calls."

"Yeah, yeah. Just go take care of your lady."

After Reese and Shea were gone, Logan sat down next to Paige. "How are you doing?"

She held up the bottle of cold water. "Better, thanks."

"You want some barbeque?"

"I don't think so. Too hot."

At that moment the announcer called another event. "That's us, darlin'," Cade said, and he and Logan clamored down the bleacher steps and jogged toward the arena.

Cade was the second cowboy up in the bull riding event, drawing a nasty looking animal that lived up to its name, Twister. The time from when bull and rider came out of the chute until the buzzer sounded was eight seconds, but felt more like eight minutes. Belle said she wasn't the least bit worried, but her hands gripped together so tightly in her lap that her knuckles were white. And when the buzzer sounded she shot out of her seat, applauding, but Paige heard her say, "Thank God."

It was after Cade was on the ground that all hell broke loose.

The bull, a huge Brahman that Belle estimated weighed well over a thousand pounds bucked wildly, spinning and twirling even after he was free of the rider. The cowboys acting as clowns couldn't distract him. The animal simply refused to settle down. Logan and three other riders were trying to herd the crazed bull toward the end of the arena, through a wide gate and into a holding pen when he stopped, spun around and charged a cowboy clown. The clown, intending to dart out of the way, accidentally tripped, falling flat out in the path of the bull. From the other side of the arena Logan rode across the path to distract the bull, but got a little too close to the angry animal. Twister turned, bucking and kicking.

His hooves struck out, catching Logan's left calf and tossing him out of the saddle. Immediately a half dozen cowboys ran across the dusty arena and surrounded the fallen rider.

Paige jumped to her feet. "He's hurt. Oh, my God, he's hurt." She would have gone tearing down to the arena if Belle hadn't stopped her.

Belle grabbed her hand. "We won't know that for sure until they— Look, he's getting up on his own. He's all right." Logan tipped his hat to the cheering crowd and she trembled with relief.

He did walk out of the arena under his own steam, but he favored his left leg, almost to the point of limping. Paige couldn't stand it. She had to make sure he was okay. She was down the bleacher steps and running toward the arena before Belle could say, "wait," or even go with her.

When she found him he was sitting on a bale of hay. He'd removed his boot and was massaging his leg. "Are you all right?" she asked, rushing up to him.

"Nothing broken," he assured her. "But I'll be madder than hell when I wake up tomorrow."

"Why?"

"'Cause it was a fool thing to do, and I'll be sore. Got too close to that bull. Didn't mean to, but it could've ruined a good horse." He grabbed his boot and leaned over to pull it on.

"Horse?" She couldn't believe his cavalier attitude. "It could've ruined a good man."

Logan looked at her from beneath the brim of his hat for a moment, then stood up and took her hat off so he could see her face, see her eyes. "Were you worried, Rusty?"

She had the feeling he was asking about a lot more than just her concern for his life and limbs. "Yes," she said, hoping she'd given the right answer to his unspoken question. Knowing she'd answered her own question of whether or not she loved him. She'd known it the instant she realized he might be hurt and confirmed it when she was assured he wasn't. The thought that he was in pain hurt her heart until it felt as if it were being torn apart.

He smiled. "That's mighty sweet. Been a while since anybody worried about me."

She blinked back tears, not wanting to make a fool out of herself in front of him. "Judging from—" she took a deep breath "—judging from the look of you, somebody needs to. You're covered with dirt, and you've got a wicked looking scrape on your forearm."

"It's nothing."

"It could become infected it it's not tended to." She reached up and brushed a piece of hay from his shoulder when what she really wanted to do was throw her arms around his neck and tell him how much she loved him. "I—I'll do it for you when we get to the house, if you want."

He wanted, all right. "Reckon you better take me home then. I need a beer, a thick steak, a bath..." He tucked a lock of hair behind her ear and she tilted her head like a kitten eager to be stroked. "...and tendin' to."

"But not necessarily in that order," Paige informed him.

He settled her hat back on her head and touched his fingers to the brim of his. "Yes, ma'am," he said in that slow, seductive drawl. "Whatever you say."

It was nearly sundown by the time they left the rodeo. A few of the cowboys had gone, but many planned to camp out, then load up and head for home the following morning. By the time Logan guided the Harley up the driveway of the farmhouse he was beginning to feel the effects of the day.

"Why don't you run a tub and soak for a while?" Paige said. "I'll shower in the downstairs bathroom, then see what I can do about that steak."

"Sounds like a hell of a deal. Oh, by the

way…uh, I know this is kind of last minute, but I was wondering, since you're going to be here… Well, I thought you might like to go to that dance tomorrow night."

"Your reunion? Are you sure?"

"Absolutely. In fact, I'm not going without you."

She smiled. "In that case, yes."

Paige watched him slowly climb the stairs. So much for her plan of a little tender loving care, she thought. It certainly looked like it would have to wait. Disappointed but not disheartened, she focused on needs of a more immediate nature. Clean body and full stomach. By the time Logan came back downstairs a half hour later, she had showered, changed into a long tiered skirt and a form-fitting T-shirt that came to her waist.

"I should refuse you service," she said as he strolled into the kitchen wearing his usual, jeans, with a bare chest and bare feet.

"What?"

"No shirt, no shoes. No service."

He laughed. "I've got a legitimate excuse."

"What's that?" She pointed to the bottle in his hand.

"Liniment." His muscles weren't nearly as sore as he wanted her to believe, but any excuse to have her hands on him was a good one. "Would you mind rubbing some of this liniment on my shoulders?"

"Of course not." The thought of refusing never entered her mind. Rub his shoulders? In a heartbeat and until her arms dropped off. Touching him was pure pleasure.

He pulled a chair away from the kitchen table and sat down, straddling it. "Thanks."

Paige filled her palm with the liniment, rubbed her hands together, then began working the liquid over his shoulders and back. Touching him felt so good she had to bite back a sigh of pleasure. And now that she knew she loved him, the pleasure doubled.

Logan felt no such restriction. "Hmm. Feels wonderful." His head lolled forward to rest on the back of the chair, giving her greater access to his neck.

With fingers splayed, Paige massaged his knotted muscles, loving the heat and texture of his skin. She worked, kneading, rubbing all across his back, shoulders, down his arms. And when she found a particularly tender spot, a place requiring a little extra attention, he let her know.

"Oh, God, that...feels...so good."

Her fingers worked his lower back. "Ah...yeah. Just a little...lower?" Her hand dipped low enough that the tips of her fingers disappeared inside the elastic waistband of his underwear. She pressed hard on his spine. "Right there. Yeah."

By now Paige's breathing wasn't so steady. The more she touched, the more she wanted to touch and slowly the touching changed. No longer content with massaging she began rubbing lightly, caressing really. While her hands stroked the slight hollow in his lower back she ached to put her lips there. Would he be shocked or would he moan? When her hands slid across his back just below his shoulder blades she wanted to keep moving them around until she touched his nipples. Would they respond as hers did? As they were responding even now? When she ran her fingers from the base of his spine to his neck then into his hair, she wanted to pull his head back and rain hot, wet kisses over his face, his neck. And what would he do then? All the things she wanted him to do? All the wonderful wicked, deliciously sensual things she longed for him to do?

"You once told me," she said, her voice raspy and sultry, "anytime a woman wanted you all she had to do was say so."

Logan went absolutely still. "I remember."

She walked around the chair so that she faced him, then she put her hands on either side of his head and slowly lifted until he saw her face. No timidity. No flirting. No mistake. She looked straight into his gorgeous blue eyes and said, "I'm saying so."

8

"PAIGE—"

"In case I didn't make myself clear… I want you."

Gently, he wrapped his fingers around her wrists, lifting her hands as he rose from the chair.

"I heard you." Then in one motion he shoved the chair away with his leg and pulled her into his arms. If she thought she was prepared for the heat, the scalding power of his kiss, she was wrong.

This was no careful seduction. It was savage male hunger, the feast long overdue. His fingers plowed through her hair, holding her prisoner for his kiss as he ravaged her mouth. She surrendered. Unconditionally.

One hand at the back of her head, the other moved over her shoulder, down her back to her waist. His hand slipped under the little T-shirt to bare skin. To that sweet, tantalizing little curve he'd once admired, holding her, or holding on to her, he wasn't sure which. All he knew was that she wasn't close enough and he didn't want to let her go. Not now, not ever. Want stoked the fires of need and his mouth moved over hers, no longer seeking, but demanding. As if her body was acutely tuned to that need, she shifted, trying to get closer, needing to get closer, answering his need with her own. When she moaned ever so softly, ever so sexily, Logan almost lost control. Carefully, still kissing her, he started toward the stairs, taking her with him. He clasped his arm around her waist holding her tight against him, lifting her just enough so that the apex of her thighs pressed against the hard ridge of his erection.

"Can't stop," he said, even as his mouth devoured hers, nibbling, sucking, "kissing you."

"Then…don't."

They made it to the stairs, took two steps up, then he stopped too quickly, almost losing his balance. Not wanting to break the embrace even long enough to walk up stairs, he compensated by going down on one knee, laying her gently back onto the carpeted step. For the first time since his lips touched hers he drew back enough to look into her eyes. His heated gaze traveled down her slender body then back while his hand slid beneath the form-fitting T-shirt to cup her breast. She gasped, instinctively arching her back.

"I have to see you…taste you," he whispered, his voice raw with need. When he reached for the hem of her T-shirt she assisted by lifting her arms so he could pull the garment over her head. He tossed it over the banister, not caring where it landed, then he unhooked her sexy little lace bra. It, too, sailed over the banister as he took one of her nipples into his mouth. He sucked strongly at her until the sweet tension was almost unbearable, then he relented, using his tongue ever so gently, maddeningly, until she reached up and pressed his head closer, needing more, wanting more. Giving in to the heat of his mouth, to the mounting heat of her own body, instinctively, she thrust her hips up. Her leg slid up his denim-clad thigh and he grounded his teeth to keep from taking her right there on the step.

"Help me, baby. We got to get to a bed."

"Kiss me again," she begged, reaching for him.

"Oh, don't worry. I'm going to kiss you sense-less in about five seconds. But not here." He put both his hands under her arms, lifting her almost to her feet, which brought her soft, satiny breasts so close to his mouth he had to look away or fall apart. He carried her the rest of the way upstairs, into his bedroom and over to the old-fashioned four-poster bed.

Then he made good on his promise to kiss her senseless.

While he held her to him with one hand and pulled her skirt off with the other, he kissed the corner of her mouth, her chin, her cheek. While he slipped a hand beneath the waistband of her panties and pushed them down over her hips, he planted tiny kisses over her delectable neck to the enticing swell of her breasts. And while he unsnapped his jeans, pushing down denim and cotton at the same time, he gave light kisses, tender kisses. Soft and slow, hard and fast.

But when she put her hands on his buttocks, pulled him against her and began rotating her hips, he kissed her long, hard and deep.

Wild with the raging need to be inside her, he

fumbled in the watch pocket of his jeans for the foil-wrapped condom, kissing her mouth all the while. Unable to stand the sweet torment another minute, he pushed her down onto the bed and quickly sheathed his penis in the condom. Then clasping both hands around her waist, he pulled her to the edge of the mattress.

"Wrap your legs around me," he said fiercely.

She moaned, reaching for him, and as her long luscious legs slid around his hips and tightened, he drove into her in one deep thrust.

She cried out, arching her back, her fingers digging into the edge of the pliant mattress. Caught between the cushiony soft bed and his powerful, hard thrusts, she abandoned herself to the double assault on her body, her senses driving her to a kind of wildness she'd never dreamed possible. Her hips rolled, undulating a rhythm with his as the heat and tension gathered, tightened to an unbearable pleasure that was almost pain. He thrust deep and hard while she writhed beneath him until finally the world splintered into a glory of white-hot passion and she screamed his name. Then he followed her into the explosion, his head thrown back, his hips jerking in completion.

The room came slowly back into focus as he picked her up, flipped the quilt back and settled her into the downy softness of the bed. They lay together quietly for long moments, arms around each other, bodies close together. Finally, Paige lifted her head from his shoulder and placed soft kisses all along his jaw, then drew back to look into his eyes. Smiling, she ran a hand through his hair. "Wonderful," she said with a sigh.

"You can say that again."

She snuggled into his shoulder again. "Wonderful. Wonderful," she muttered against his neck.

"I've got a confession," he said.

"Don't care."

He pulled back and looked at her. "A man that's just had the most incredible sex of his life with you says he's got a confession, and you don't care?"

She shook her head.

"Aw, c'mon." He grinned. "Aren't you even curious?"

"Nope. I don't care if *you're* an ax murderer or married with a dozen kids, as long as you can make love to me like this." She raised up on one elbow. "You know I wasn't serious about the wife and— The most incredible sex of your life?"

"Wondered when that would click in." He kissed her mouth, her neck.

"Okay, so what's...mmm...the confession?"

He stroked her breast, plumping her fullness, rubbing his thumb back and forth across her still-sensitive nipple. "You have the most gorgeous, devastating legs."

"Thank... Oh-h..." His mouth replaced his thumb and she started to move restlessly.

"I fantasized about your legs. Wrapped around me. Spread wide for me." He pulled her beneath him as she did just that, but he didn't enter her right away. First he wanted to explore.

Before their kisses had been all heat and fire.

Fast and furious. Now he took his slow, sweet time kissing her, acquainting himself with the taste and texture of her mouth. Educating himself with the satin softness of her skin. His lips explored the slant of her cheek, pressing tiny kisses all the way to her soft, succulent earlobe and discovered a spot in the hollow of her neck so sensitive the touch of his mouth brought forth a shuddering sigh. He kissed her closed eyelids, her forehead, finally returning to her lips, parted, waiting. He rewarded her patience, giving her long tender kisses that turned her legs to water. Courting her with we've-got-all-night kind of kisses that left her body weak and her mind drugged with the most erotic images.

She loved it, but it wasn't enough. Her hips pumped against him, eager for his full, deep possession of her body. "Logan, please…"

"Easy, darlin'. We've got time."

"But I want—" She gasped when she felt him probe her hot, slick entrance. "Yes, yes."

"That what you want?" He teased her, almost giving her what she wanted, but not quite.

"*Yes.* But…more."

"Easy, easy."

She twisted against the sheets knowing there would be no ease until he was inside her. "More. Logan…please."

"And you'll have it, just—"

"No." She wasn't willing to wait another second. As she hooked her legs around his thighs she raked her nails down his back to cup his buttock, pulling him into her and rising to meet him at the same time.

Her wild response stripped away the last of his control and he gladly acceded to her demand, giving her everything she wanted and more. They were lost in each other, lost in the heat and power, lost in the wild storm of passion until they found their way to the edge, then over into the sweet oblivion they both craved.

And then he held her. Just held her, as he'd longed to do from the day they met.

SOMETIME IN THE NIGHT, Logan woke and simply stared at her sleeping so peacefully beside him. So beautiful. So passionate. He'd thought once he'd satisfied himself with her it would be enough. But it wasn't. Even while she gave herself so passionately, even while he poured himself into her, it hadn't been enough. And now, the more he gazed at her, the more aroused he became; in fact, he was hard again. On the verge of trying to convince himself not to wake her, he looked down to find her staring at him. Without a word, she put both hands behind his neck, drawing his head down for a long, hungry, demanding kiss as she began to move sensuously under him.

Several hours later, Logan woke and realized he was alone in the bed. Then he saw Paige. Wearing his bathrobe, she sat curled up in his grandmother's rocking chair busy with her sketch pad and pencil. She looked sweet and sexy and right in his room. Then, as if she sensed him watching her, she lifted her head and smiled at him. Just smiled. But it had a profound effect on him. Something isolated, something locked away inside him for God knows how long, was suddenly free. A gift from Paige, courtesy of her loving smile. He was about to say something to her when the phone rang. He reached to the nightstand and picked up the phone. "Walker," he said.

She whispered, "I can leave if you want—"

"Don't move," he ordered, then said to the caller, "Hello."

"You talkin' to a woman?" Rick Conner asked.

Logan propped himself up on one elbow and smiled at Paige. "Oh, yeah."

"Why you sly devil—"

"Slow down, partner."

"—and here I was worried you'd be lonely. Who is she?"

"Rick."

"Yeah?"

"What do you want?" Logan motioned for her to come back to bed, but she grinned and shook her head.

"You're not going to tell me who she is, are you?"

"Bull's-eye."

"Oops. I didn't interrupt something, did I?"

"Double your insurance, Conner. You're gonna need it when I get my hands on you. I'll call you back." And he hung up. Stilling watching her, he stretched his powerful shoulders, then lay back, his hands behind his head. "How long have you been up?"

"Around sunrise."

He glanced at the sketch pad. "You've been busy. Doing what?"

"Something I've wanted to do practically since we met. Capturing you on paper."

"Can I see?"

"Nope." She hugged the pad to her chest. "It's not finished."

"I'll tell you something else that's not finished." He patted the empty space beside him.

Paige set her artist's tools aside, walked to the edge of the bed. "Wouldn't you like some breakfast?" He shook his head. "Coffee?" He shook his head again. "Let me think." She climbed onto the bed. "Don't want anything to eat. Or drink. You've had…well, some rest. What else could you possibly want?"

His gaze seared her with that blue flame of desire she now knew so well. Of course, she knew what he wanted, but she needed to hear him speak the words as she had spoken them last night. Slowly, she rose to her knees and untied the sash of the robe, allowing it to fall open. With the slightest shrug of first one creamy shoulder then the other, the robe slipped from her slender body. Gloriously naked, she said, "Tell me what you want."

Until then he'd remained unmoving except for his hot-eyed gaze. Now, he threw back the sheet revealing his hard-muscled body and harder erection. Then he, too, rose to his knees, close enough that her already responsive nipples brushed his chest.

She swayed back and forth, brushing against him, teasing, sweetly tormenting. "Tell me," she demanded, trying hard to stay in control with him mere inches away.

He fisted his hand in her hair, gently tugging until her face, her breathtaking face, was in perfect position for the voracious kisses he planned. "I want you," he groaned.

"Show me," she whispered, a startling counterpoint to his almost guttural moan as she pushed him down, straddling his powerful body.

THEY MISSED BREAKFAST.

While Paige was downstairs opening a can of soup and building some sandwiches for lunch, Logan called his partner from the bedroom phone.

"Hey, there," he said as soon as Rick answered. "Sorry I had to cut you short before."

"No problem, Tex. You got a few minutes?"

"Yeah. But this better be important."

"This is not, I repeat, not a call for you to bail me out. I need to get hold of your golf-pro friend, Shawn Booker. He's been a reliable source for you in the past and I need to reach him."

"His home number and the number for the country club where he works are in the computer. That's all I've got."

At other end of the phone, Rick sighed. "I was afraid of that."

"What do you want with Shawn?"

"That case—the one I tried to tell you about the morning you left—is going to require some special handling. We're talking gentry. Top of the pile. And top dollar for us, I might add. I knew Booker ran with that crowd and thought he might have some information. And since I know you're dying to ask about the details but that stubborn streak of yours won't let you, I'll tell you. Seems one of Denver's crème de la crème is missing. The Davenport heiress did a little disappearing act."

"Kidnapped?"

"Naw. Found the boyfriend between the sheets with her maid of honor the night before the I-dos. She traded cars with a friend that was leaving town and hit the road, Jack. Naturally, the family wants it all kept out of the papers."

"Naturally." There was a long pause before Logan said, "By the way, what color was the car?"

"A forest-green Jag. See, I knew you couldn't turn off that ex-cop head of yours. And before you ask, the tag is personalized…" Logan knew what Rick was going to say before he finished the sentence. "RG ONE."

"Uh, listen, Rick, I hate to cut and run, but I'm kind of busy—"

"Never thought I'd live to see the day. The lady with the sexy voice must have your full attention."

"Yeah," Logan said. "She sure does."

In more ways than one, he thought, after talking to Rick. Enough that he couldn't ignore the evidence. Davenport heiress. Disappearing act. Traded cars with a friend who was leaving town, then hit the road. And last, but not least—a green Jaguar with the tag, RG ONE.

His long-legged redhead, his Paige, was a missing heiress. The sexy, sultry woman in his bed last night and this morning was from one of the richest families in Denver. Logan couldn't quite take it all in, but he knew it had to be true. Either that or it was the biggest coincidence in history, and he didn't believe in coincidence.

Paige Davenport.

He had a runaway on his hands.

So many things made sense now. Why she'd been driving a borrowed car. Why she'd given him a phony name, and why she'd looked so out of her element trying to fend off two road bandits. No wonder she didn't want to contact any of her friends. Or her family. Rick had said she found her fiancé in bed with her maid of honor the night before the wedding. That was enough to send anybody heading for the hills. Obviously, she'd turned to Regina Fox for help, and then ol' Regi had gone off to party thinking Paige was set.

He understood and even sympathized with her reason for not going through with a wedding to a worthless, cheating jerk. And he could even see where she might want a little time alone after such an ordeal. But why would she leave all those millions for a job in an art gallery in Houston? Unless she really wouldn't. Maybe her little jaunt to Houston and her proclamation of freedom ran more along the lines of a temper tantrum than a bid for independence.

Old anger and resentment coiled inside him like a poisonous snake. That description certainly fit his money-grubbing, can't-do-without-luxury ex-wife. Paige had been born with a platinum spoon in her mouth. She came from, and was accustomed to, the same kind of luxury as the selfish, self-centered Cindi. His hands curled into fists when he remembered her betrayal. Then he glanced at the bed and another memory, a more recent one, had him taking a deep breath. Paige wasn't Cindi, and he had no right to tar her with the same brush. There wasn't a selfish bone in Paige's delectable body. And as for money, she'd never asked him for anything and, even when he'd offered, she hadn't taken excessively. In fact, she'd acted like a kid at a candy counter when she discovered that resale shop. Looking at the smile on her face, anyone would have thought she'd struck gold instead of second-hand clothes. She was working off her debt by being his housekeeper for God's sake, a job for which she was totally unqualified, but one she had tackled with determination. She'd never asked for a free ride.

Logan smiled. Except for last night. Only she'd been the rider.

No, that woman, the woman downstairs waiting for him, wasn't self-centered or mercenary. She wasn't anything like his ex-wife. Thank God.

Because he thought he was falling in love with her.

The thought first popped into his head when he woke up and saw her sketching him. She'd been so intent on her work, so focused…and so beautiful with the sunlight streaming in behind her, backlighting her hair like a golden halo. Only, she was no angel. She was all woman. And when she'd looked at him and smiled it was almost as if he'd heard a click in his head. And maybe his heart. Everything clicked, settled into the right place. As if he'd been waiting for her smile to make his life fit together the way it was supposed to. Like the last piece of a puzzle.

But, he reminded himself, it was his puzzle. Just because Paige wasn't like his ex didn't mean she had turned her back on Davenport money and power. From the beginning, he'd sensed she was running away from something or somebody, and now he knew. So the boyfriend was a world-class bastard. Even if she never forgave him and ditched the marriage, didn't mean she wanted to ditch her family. She'd been born to a kind of life-style that, to him, appeared meaningless, but that was only his perspective, not hers. He believed her when she said she wanted her own life, but that kind of money was a powerful temptation. What if she decided to go back? What if he fell in love with her and she left the way his ex-wife had?

He'd been hurt when Cindi left and a lot of the pain centered around his pride. But something told him losing Paige would be a whole lot different. If he let himself love her and she walked away, she'd be walking away with his heart.

"CADE AND BELLE are picking us up at seven," Logan said, pouring himself a glass of iced tea. He'd been painting the garage since lunch and his face, arms and raggedy T-shirt were sweaty and speckled with paint.

Paige glanced at the clock. "That doesn't give me much time."

"It'll take you four hours to get ready?"

"No. I don't have anything to wear to a dance,

so I thought I might go back to that resale shop, and—"

"You want to go shopping?"

"Yesterday they had an inexpensive little dress that would be perfect for tonight. I know it's an imposition, but—"

"But that's okay so long as you get a new dress."

She stared at him, stunned at the sharpness in his voice. If he was too busy to drive her, she could walk—it wasn't that far—but there was more to it than just taking up his time. "Logan, what's wrong?"

"Nothing's wrong. I just don't have the time or the money for shopping."

She simply stood and stared, unable to believe this was the same man she'd made love to. Until a moment ago she'd felt closer to him than anyone in her whole life. Clearly, he was angry, but why?

"All right," she said, truly confused. "Belle offered to—"

"No. You're not going to have Belle chauffeur you around."

She took a step toward him. "Logan, something is wrong."

"I told you. Nothing's wrong."

Suddenly, it occurred to her that he had been unusually subdued since the phone call from his partner. Could he have received some disturbing news about their business? He'd been so generous, she'd never questioned whether or not he could afford to be. She knew from living with her overachieving father that so much of a man's self-worth was tied up in his career. And the usual yardstick for measuring a successful career was money. She had wanted to look good in front of his friends and former classmates and now she was ashamed of her self-centered attitude.

"I—I'm sorry. I only wanted—"

"I don't want to talk about it anymore." He banged the empty glass down on the counter, yanked a small towel out of his back pocket and wiped his face and arms. "Going to the hardware store," he said, and walked out.

The slamming of the back door reverberated through her entire body, ending with a dull ache in her heart. Something was terribly wrong. One minute he was the handsome, sexy man she loved and the next he was biting her head off. He acted as if all she cared about was…his money.

Exactly like his ex-wife.

Of course. It all made sense now. Paige started to go after him, then changed her mind. She would just have to trust Logan's analytical mind, his ex-cop legacy of observation. His past was nipping at him and he would see that. As for money for the dress, she had an idea that would satisfy his pride and her desire to make him proud, but she had to hurry. She called the resale shop to see if the dress she wanted was still there, made another call, then headed for town. Forty-five minutes later Paige had completed her mission, and luck was with her because she had just walked in the house when she heard the Harley coming into the driveway. She ran upstairs and stashed her purchases. Logan was waiting for her when she came down.

"It's, uh, about what happened earlier…" Looking down, he shifted his weight from one foot to the other. "Well, I sorta lost it, and, uh…"

He was struggling so hard to apologize she decided to have pity on him. "Acted like a jerk?"

He looked up, surprised to see her smiling and his heart swelled two sizes. She was going to forgive him. Thank God. "More like a first-class ass."

"That'll work."

"I'm sorry, Paige," he said with a sigh of relief. "I had no right to talk to you like that. I'm not trying to excuse my sorry behavior, but for a minute—"

"I know. I sounded like your ex-wife, didn't I?"

"Yeah. It was a knee-jerk reaction and I'm sorry."

Paige walked to him, slipping her arms around his neck. "Well, at least we agree you got the jerk part right."

"So, will you forgive me?"

"Eventually. After I've decided on sufficient punishment, like…oh, making you my personal love slave."

"In that case, Red, punish to your heart's content." He kissed her softly, sweetly, thankfully. Then he took her in his arms and held her. Just held her. "How about we skip the dance and go straight to the punishment."

"Not on your life." She drew back and looked

into his eyes. "I've got a little confession of my own."

He raised one eyebrow. "I'm all ears."

"I walked into town while you were gone and, before you say anything, I took one of my outfits to the resale shop and worked out a trade."

"Now I really do feel like a low-down heel."

"You should." She couldn't resist a little dig. "But you'll feel better when you see me in this dress."

"Yeah?"

"Oh, yeah."

WHEN HE SAW her in the dress he felt something all right, but he wouldn't exactly call it better. Stunned—the any-woman-looking-that-good-should-be-locked-up variety of stunned.

"So?" She stood in the middle of her bedroom wearing an emerald-green silk slipdress, the hemline just barely at midthigh. The rest was just her. Slender arms and those mouth-watering legs and a pair of strappy high-heeled shoes. "What do you think?"

"I think—" Logan cleared his throat "—I may need to strap on my granddaddy's old holster and Colt .45 'cause I might end up defending your honor. Darlin', you look spectacular."

Smiling, she did a slow turn for him. "Told you you'd like it."

"The only way I'd like that dress any better, is if you *weren't* wearing it."

She laughed. "Good things come to those who wait."

He was about ready to say to hell with waiting when he heard a car horn. "Our ride is here."

She picked up a small black evening bag. "I'm ready."

With his hand at the small of her back, Logan ushered her out of the bedroom and downstairs. "That's the trouble. So am I."

Cade was waiting for them in a shiny red Suburban.

"Where's everybody else?" Logan asked.

"At the hospital. Shea went into labor about an hour ago. I had Belle drive them to the hospital in Lubbock. Reese was a wreck."

"You should have called," Paige insisted.

"Well, no tellin' how long she'll be in labor. Seemed like days when I was waitin' for Chance to be born. Anyway, I didn't wanna leave y'all afoot, so I figured you could drop me at the hospital and keep the Suburban until tomorrow."

After a thirty-minute delay during which Cade argued them out of staying at the hospital, Logan and Paige finally arrived at the Sweetwater Springs High School gym, appropriately decorated for the reunion.

"I don't recognize any of these people," Logan said to Paige as they tried to read name tags. At that moment the band hit the downbeat on "Waltz Across Texas." "Now, there's something I do recognize." He took Paige by the hand and led her onto the dance floor, then into his arms.

"I'm liking that dress better with every passing minute." He pulled her closer and bent to nibble on her ear as they swayed to a two-step. "Hey, you aren't wearing your sparkly little diamonds," he said, noting she'd substituted tiny pearl drop earrings.

"Oh, uh, I just decided they didn't go with this dress. And speaking of finery, you don't look too bad yourself."

"Thank you, ma'am."

He wore a navy-blue Western-cut suit, an immaculate white Western shirt and eelskin boots almost the rusty-red color of her hair. Glancing up at him she toyed with the snaps down the front of his shirt.

"I wouldn't do that if I were you."

"Why not?"

"You pop one snap on my shirt and I may have to haul you off to Cade's truck. Ever made it in a back seat, Red?"

She almost missed a beat in the slow two-step as the image of naked bodies and steamed windows came to mind. "There's a first time for everything."

When the music stopped, they headed back to find a table and, suddenly, Logan stopped so fast Paige had to grab his arm to keep her balance. He was staring at someone off to their right and the look on his face was hard as granite.

"Logan? What is it? What's the matter?"

"That woman in the black dress."

Paige saw an attractive woman with dark hair wearing a stunning evening dress that she was almost certain was an original. A bit much for a high-school reunion, she thought, but to each her own. "The woman standing next to the older man? Do you know her?"

"Yeah. She's my ex-wife."

9

PAIGE LOOKED AT Logan's ex-wife and tried very hard not to take an instant dislike to the woman that had once shared his bed. She really did try. Well, sort of. As bad as she hated to admit it—and she hated it a lot—the woman was a stunner.

"You—you didn't know she was going to be here?"

"Hell, no. Cindi's the last person I expected to see. She only went to school here her senior year and couldn't wait to go off to college in Austin. She wanted bigger and better things."

Like you, Paige thought. No wonder he was gun-shy when a woman started talking about money. The lady in expensive black had certainly left her mark on him. Then Paige realized Logan hadn't taken his eyes off his ex-wife since he'd spotted her. Just how deep was that mark? she wondered. Was it possible he still felt something for her? Sometimes there was a fine line between love and hate.

"Do you want to leave?"

He looked down at her. "Do you?"

She loved his eyes, always so intense and expressive, but at the moment they were dark with an emotion she couldn't name. And it frightened her. "I—I want what you want," she said, hoping he heard the deeper message in her answer.

Logan smiled and some of the darkness left his eyes. "Right now I want to kiss you so bad it hurts, but—" he glanced around "—guess I'll have to settle for holding you." He took her hand. "C'mon, Rusty. Dance with me."

Swinging onto the floor, they mingled with the other couples. Paige wanted the music to go on forever so she would never have to leave his arms. Never have to deal with the fact of his ex-wife. When the music stopped they made their way across the crowded floor, almost colliding with another couple as they looked around for a table.

"Oh, pardon me, ma'am. I didn't..." Logan stopped.

"Well, Logan. Fancy bumping into you."

"Hello, Cindi," he replied, coolly.

"How are you?"

"Fine."

"Oh," Cindi said, as if just remembering her partner. "This is my husband, Thomas Holland. Tom, this is Logan Walker."

"Number one husband, I believe," Holland said, smiling, shaking hands. "I'm number three."

Cindi looped her arm through her husband's. "And who is this, your little wife?"

"Paige O'Neil, meet Cindi Holland."

"Hello."

"That's a charming dress, Paige, is it?"

"Thank you." A lengthy pause followed in which Paige knew she was expected to comment—favorably, no doubt—on the black gown. And as much as she would like to have kept quiet, good manners and common courtesy dictated otherwise. "That's a stunning original you're wearing. Vera Wang, isn't it?"

Cindi Holland's eyes widened in surprise for just a second before she regained her composure. "Why, yes."

"So, Walker," Tom Holland said. "Cindi's told me all about you. She mentioned you were in law enforcement, I believe."

"That was awhile back. I have a research firm in Denver."

Cindi put a hand on her husband's chest in a gesture that looked more possessive than affectionate. "Tom is a surgeon in Dallas. His practice is incredibly demanding, and we've started construction on a new state-of-the-art clinic, so we weren't certain we could make the reunion until the last minute."

"Now, sugar, don't brag," Holland said, but his own chest looked a little puffy.

"Well, if a wife can't brag on her wonderfully successful husband, who can, I'd like to know?"

Cindi Holland stood next to her current husband looking at her ex-husband, waving what she considered success in his face. The woman was clueless. Totally oblivious to the fact that when she walked away from Logan she'd traded twenty-four karat for fool's gold. Paige only hoped and prayed that Cindi Holland's loss would be her gain.

As Logan listened to his ex going on at length about the new clinic and their busy social life he looked at the two women side by side and couldn't help but compare them. But it didn't take more than a few seconds to realize there was no comparison. They might as well have put a rhinestone next to the Hope Diamond.

Sure, Cindi had the polish and shine, but that was all. She had no real life, no fire. The face and figure drew attention, but she might as well have been a mannequin for all the warmth she possessed.

On the other hand, Paige had everything.

Wearing resale clothes and the sweetest smile this side of heaven, she had more class and style than Cindi could ever hope to have. There wasn't enough money in the world to buy the kind of genuine beauty Paige possessed. She might be the Davenport heiress, but her real wealth was a gentle spirit and a loving heart.

And he didn't think he was falling in love with her; he *knew*. He was hopelessly, completely and forever in love with her.

Fate, he thought, sure surprised you when you least expected it. A week ago the last thing on his mind was love, much less marriage. Then along came a sassy redhead with lost puppy eyes that turned his life every which way but loose. She was a treasure, and now that he'd found her he didn't want to let her go. In the beginning he'd manipulated and shaded the truth to keep her near for selfish reasons. Now, he wanted her with him always, and for the only right reason. Because he loved her. And he thought, he prayed, she loved him too. But would it be enough?

Of course, sooner or later, he had to tell her he knew who she was, and that might be tricky. He made a mental note to call Rick first thing tomorrow morning and have him return the Davenport's retainer and resign from the case. He knew there was already out-of-pocket money spent that might hurt their bottom line, but he'd rather lose dollars than have Paige think he'd been shadowing her all the time.

"And what do you do, Paige?" Holland asked at the end of his wife's detailed account of their lives.

"At the moment I'm between jobs, but—"

"Paige is an artist," Logan said. "And she's incredibly talented."

Smiling, she looked up at him. "Sure you're not just saying that because you're my favorite subject?"

Logan gazed at her, so beautiful, so sweet and loving she almost took his breath away. "Because it's true," he said, wanting to tell her right then and there that he loved her, but fighting his fear that it wouldn't be enough.

Cindi glanced around. "And where are those ever-present rowdy friends of yours?"

"If you mean Cade and Reese," Paige said, "they would have been here but Reese's wife is in labor with their first child."

Cindi Holland's smile drooped slightly and there was a flash of pain in her eyes before she looked away. When she looked back, the smile was fixed and bright. "How sweet."

Any jealousy Paige had felt vanished in that moment because she had no doubt her comment had struck a tender spot in Cindi's haute couture armor. And any uncertainty she'd felt about Logan's feelings toward his ex-wife vanished in the next moment when she saw the look of pity in his eyes. Poor Cindi, she thought.

"Yeah," he said, slipping his arm around Paige's waist and pulling her to him. "They're at the hospital right now."

"Which is exactly where we should be," Paige said, looking to Logan for approval.

"Yeah. Nice to see you," he told the Hollands, leading Paige away even as he spoke. "Thanks," he said when they were out of earshot.

"For what?"

"For rescuing me. There's not enough beer in this place, maybe not the whole State of Texas, to make listening to those people for another minute bearable."

"I felt that way, but I thought you might want to talk to her."

"Don't have anything to say to her. Actually, I never did. I just didn't realize it until tonight. You know, it's funny, but she looked almost lonely when she was spouting off about what a great life she has. And I saw a look in her eyes—"

"When I mentioned Reese and Shea's baby?" He nodded. "I saw it, too."

"You know, I never thought I'd hear myself say this, but I feel sorry for her, Paige."

"So do I, but I have to confess I was a little worried at first."

"What about?"

"Oh, I thought maybe you might still have

some feelings for her, which is understandable. She was your first love.''

"I was a kid then, without the sense to realize that just because something sparkled didn't make it a diamond. Why would I even look at her when I've got the prettiest, sexiest, smartest woman in the whole place on my arm? Not a chance, Red.''

"Well, I'd be lying if I said I wasn't glad. And speaking of lying, I wasn't just making an excuse when I said I thought we should be at the hospital. They're your friends and this is an important event.''

They had walked out of the gym and were headed toward the main entrance. Logan stopped, turned her into his arms and kissed her, soundly.

"What was that for?'' she asked a little breathless.

"Because I...'' No, he wasn't going to tell her he loved her standing in the middle of the high-school foyer. She deserved better. Probably even better than him, but it was too late. He loved her too much to lose her. "Because you're right. We do belong with our friends. And because I just like kissing you.''

Fifteen minutes later they walked into the maternity waiting room and joined Cade and Belle in the vigil. When they left seven hours later it was still dark, with just a faint promise of the new day on the horizon. Reese and Shea were the proud parents of small, but healthy, and of course, beautiful twin girls.

"Don't know about you,'' Logan said as they

walked up the stairs of the dark farmhouse, "but this baby stuff is nerve-racking, not to mention downright exhausting."

"Hmm. Who would have thought sitting around a waiting room for hours would be so wearing?" He'd given her his suit coat because the waiting room had been so cold. Now she slipped out of it and lay it on the chaise lounge in the corner of the bedroom.

Logan pulled her into his arms. "Sleepy?"

"My body's tired, but my mind won't turn off."

"We need to get some shut-eye."

"I suppose."

He drew back and looked at her. "Suppose? You know what time it is?"

"Late. No, early. Who cares? We've just been part of something really awesome and I feel this strange sort of energy."

"Energy? You just said you were tired."

"I know, and it'll probably hit me like a ton of bricks in a few minutes, but..." He'd long since removed his tie and popped the top two snaps of his shirt. She played with the remaining snaps as she'd done the night before.

"But what?"

"Don't you want to...unwind before we go to sleep?"

"Unwind, huh?"

She popped two more snaps, pushing his shirt open. "We could give each other a massage."

"We could—" his breath hit the back of his throat when her lips touched his bare chest "— do that." He knew where this was heading. Not that he objected, but this time he wanted it to be different. This time he wanted her to feel treasured, loved. "But I'd rather..."

She gazed up at him, her lips parted just waiting to be kissed. "Rather what?"

"Make love to you."

She caught her breath. He'd never used the word, "love" before. "Oh yes," she whispered as his lips claimed hers. "Please."

While he kissed her deeply, thoroughly, he eased one strap of the dress over her shoulder, then the other. And then, gently, he touched her, stroking her soft, warm breasts. And while his hands caressed, his thumb moved over and around her nipple, slowly, maddeningly. Wonderfully. Until it was almost more than she could bear, yet couldn't bear for him to stop. A lazy heat spread through her body, soft as a sultry June night but with the promise of a summer storm.

When she sighed into his mouth, he thought it was the sweetest sound on earth, fueling the endless kiss. He couldn't get enough of her mouth, so warm, so willing. He lingered to nibble on her lower lip, then kissed her again and again, until finally his senses were spinning with the taste of her. Slowly, his hands moved down over her body and gathered fistfuls of her dress. He leaned back just enough to pull it over her head then sent it sailing across the room. The panty hose quickly followed the dress and, almost before she could whisper his name, he laid her back on the bed. And then he made slow, sweet love to her, worshipping her body with tender touches, soft murmurs and soul-stirring kisses.

He made it last until they were both breathless and mindless with need. Then and only then did he fill her. They moved together so smoothly, so perfectly, their bodies one. When she cried out her pleasure, she cried out her love for him as well. The thrill of her declaration went through him like lightning and he poured himself into her. As they floated back to earth from the soaring pleasure, totally spent, he held her close and kissed her temple. Moments later, after he'd caught his breath, he said, "I love you."

When she didn't stir he looked down and realized she was asleep. God, she was so beautiful. And not just pretty to look at, but beautiful clear through. "I love you, Rusty. More than I ever thought I could love anybody. You're the best thing that's happened to me." There was a right and wrong to every situation, and he was walking a thin line. Right was telling her the truth, despite the risk. But the greatest wrong would be losing her. He brushed a lock of hair from her cheek. "I'm scared to death," he admitted. Then carefully, he picked up her delicate hand, kissing her fingertips, her palm. "My heart's right here, sweetheart. Hang on to it," he whispered as he drifted into sleep beside her.

PAIGE WOKE TO bright sunlight and a growling stomach. Beside her Logan still slept deeply. So deeply he didn't even stir when she slipped out of bed and went downstairs. It felt like morning but the hour was well past noon and she hadn't eaten since before the dance last night. Last night, Paige thought, pouring herself a glass of milk. Last night had been the most beautiful, thrilling, wonderful night of her life. She closed her eyes and sighed with pure pleasure at the memory. Never in her life had she felt so treasured, cherished. So...loved?

Logan was a miracle.

In a short time he'd changed her, changed her life. She was so hopelessly in love with him that sometimes just looking at him made her want to cry. For the first time she saw a future filled with love. A future with Logan.

Yes, she was dreamy-eyed. How could she not be after the way he'd made love to her last night? Today her heart was so full she wanted to throw her arms around the whole world and give it a great big hug. Everything was wonderful. Everybody was wonderful.

Including her parents?

Yes, she decided, tears filling her eyes. Including her parents.

And that was the true miracle of loving Logan. It had opened her eyes and her heart. A week ago she'd thought she had to separate herself totally from her family in order to be free. Now she knew the only real freedom was in loving. Sometimes there was, indeed, a fine line between love and hate, particularly between parent and child. She'd withheld her love from them because she felt it could never have been returned equally. But love wasn't a balance sheet. There was no measure, no way to quantitate the amount, or the depth of love. It was a gift. To another, to your-

self. And in their own way, her parents loved
her. It was up to her to find a place for that love
in her life. Granted, it would take time and she
might always struggle with her mother's domi-
nant personality, but she could even face that
now. She didn't regret leaving, nor did she intend to go running back. Whatever happened,
she would live her life the way she wanted. But
she had hurt them, she realized, and herself.
How childish she'd been. It was a wonder Logan
had put up with her at all.

It was time to make things right.

She walked to the phone and made a collect
call to Denver.

"Paige?" her mother said, the instant the con-
nection was made. "Oh, thank God. Are you all
right?"

"I'm fine, Mother."

"We've been so worried."

"That's why I'm calling. I'm sorry."

"It's all right. We'll talk about everything
when you get home—"

"Mother—"

"Do you have money for a plane ticket? If not,
I can call—"

"Mother! I'm not coming home."

"What are you talking about? Of course,
you're coming home."

Paige gathered every last scrap of her courage,
knowing she was going to need it. "Mother, I
know running out the way I did put you and
Dad in a bad situation. I could, and should, have
handled it better. But that doesn't change the fact

that I'm not going to marry Randal. And I'm not coming back to Denver."

"Now, Paige," her mother said, in her best censuring tone. "I can understand how upset you were over Randal's…indiscretion, but this is not how we handle things. There are people to consider other than yourself. After all—"

"I'm a Davenport," Paige finished for her.

"Yes."

"And there's the scandal to think of."

"Well, yes. Do you have any idea what your father and I have been through? Just trying to trace you has been a nightmare."

"I'm sure it has. And I'm sure you've spent considerable time and money. How many private detectives are on my trail?"

"Two separate agencies. The Hillard Company has at least a dozen men working on the case, and Rick Conner of Denver Investigations—"

"Who did you say?"

"Rick Conner. His partner is the one who found Andrew and Cici Wilson's granddaughter when their nanny abducted her several months ago."

The name Rick Conner kept bouncing around in Paige's head, but she couldn't quite place it.

"Paige? Are you still there?"

"Yes, Mother. You can call off your investigators now. I'm in a little town called Sweetwater Springs, Texas, and—"

"Texas? Why on earth would you go to Texas?"

"Because it's where I want to be. And, please,

don't think you can come down here and change my mind."

"I don't want to change your mind—"

"Yes, you do. You want me to fit into the mold you created, to live the life you planned for me."

"What's so terrible about your life?"

"Nothing, but it's not mine. It's a reenactment of yours. Please, try to understand."

"Well, I don't. You've had every advantage. Every opportunity and I fail to see any reason—"

"Exactly. You can't see my point of view and I'm not going to argue with you, Mother. I love you and Father and I want us to have a relationship, but I can't...I won't live with you again under any circumstances. Now you can rant and rave about it, or you can accept it gracefully. The choice is yours."

Her mother sighed. Paige recognized it as one of her "I surrender, but only temporarily" sighs. Finally, after several seconds of silence, her mother said, "I suppose if we come to Texas you'll just dash off again."

"No. I'm not running from you or anyone else ever again. I'll be here for another four or five days until my new job starts in Houston." She fudged a little on the job, but she knew if her mother saw one tiny crack in her plan she'd jump on it in a heartbeat.

"Houston! But—"

"I'll be working in a gallery, and I hope, using some of my spare time to work with kids again. As soon as I'm settled, I'd like you and Dad to come for a visit." That last statement took more courage than she realized she had, but it was true.

Another long silence on her mother's end of the line. "Obviously you've given this some thought."

"For a long time."

"I—I've never heard you quite so…adamant."

"I suggest you get used to it, Mother." Paige took a deep, cleansing breath. "It's the way things will be from now on."

A few moments later she said goodbye to her mother and felt as if a weight had been lifted from her shoulders. It would definitely take time for her parents to accustom themselves to the new Paige, and they might never fully understand her, but she could live with that. In time, so would they.

At least now she could tell Logan the truth. Her mother would call off the dogs, so to speak, and she wouldn't have to worry about private detectives lurking around every corner. Thinking about that, the name Rick Conner came to mind again, tugging at her memory. Maybe she'd met him at a charity function or a party? But she couldn't put a face with the name. Her mother had said he had a partner, maybe…

On her way back upstairs, suddenly Paige stopped, memories popping in her mind like flashbulbs. Memories of comments Logan had made about his work.

We collect data for our clients.

My partner, Rick Conner, is handling the business. That's how I'm able to take this time off.

Double your insurance, Conner.

It couldn't be the same Rick Conner. It just couldn't. That would mean... No, Logan wasn't... He couldn't be...

But even while denial rang in her mind, an icy dread clutched her heart. What if it was true? What if Logan had been keeping tabs on her all along?

Suddenly, she saw things she'd never questioned before in a whole new light. Things like him giving her money so freely. Why not be generous when it would all be reimbursed? Things like asking her to work off the money she owed him. What easier way to keep an eye on her? Things like the fact that he carried a gun, which seemed perfectly logical considering he used to be...

An ex-cop.

What better background for a private investigator?

Numb, Paige sat down on the stairs and leaned her head against the wall. She didn't want to believe it. Oh, God, how she hated to believe it. Had he been lying to her from the moment they met? Had every kiss, every word been just one big, fat lie? "No," she whispered. "Please, no."

She felt dejected, defeated, exactly the same way she'd felt the night she walked in on Randal, only ten times worse. A hundred times worse. Finally, she pushed herself to her feet and continued upstairs. To pack.

It didn't take long and, thankfully, Logan hadn't awakened. She had almost finished when she remembered her sketch pad was in his bed-

room. Just leave it, she thought. It wasn't
worth...

Suddenly, Paige stopped. Wasn't worth what?
Those sketches were some of the best work she'd
ever done and she had almost walked away from
them without a backward glance. No, not
walked away. Run away. That was her pattern,
had always been her pattern. She had run rather
than face Randal's infidelity. She had run rather
than stand up to her parents. Even her little teen-
age rebellions were nothing more than running
away from home in one form or another.

And now she was running from Logan. From
confronting his treachery.

*I'm not running from you or anyone else ever
again.*

She'd said those words to her mother less than
a half hour ago, never realizing she would have
to stand behind them so soon. As she'd done the
night she ran to Regi for help, the more she
thought about what happened, the angrier she
became. In a way, that, too, was childish. No
more, she decided. She'd packed her last bag,
run her last mile. She intended to confront Logan, but not while she was mad. When she told
him exactly what she thought of him, she would
do it with a clear head, her emotions under control.

Paige walked into the bedroom where Logan
lay sleeping, and stood at the foot of the bed just
looking at him for several minutes. "Damn you,
Logan Walker," she whispered. "And damn me
for falling in love with you." Then she

crossed the room, picked up the loose sketches and put them inside her sketch pad.

The sound of paper rustling woke Logan and he sat up in bed, smiling. "Mornin', Rusty." Then he glanced at the clock. "Guess afternoon is more appropriate." When she didn't answer him or turn around, he frowned. "What are you doing with your sketches?"

Finally, she faced him. "You're the private detective. You figure it out." And she walked out of the room.

10

"AW, HELL!" Logan jumped out of bed and into his jeans, trying to zip them as he ran after her. "Paige," he yelled, expecting her to be out of the house and walking to God knew where by the time he got downstairs. She was standing at the kitchen door, car keys in her hand. His bare feet almost skidded on the floor he stopped so fast. "Thank God, I thought you'd gone."

"Oh, make no mistake. I'm leaving this house, but not Sweetwater Springs. At least not until I've had a chance to tell you what a rotten, no good, lying son-of-a—"

"Easy, Rusty. I know you're mad and you've got a right to be."

"I haven't even gotten started."

"If you'll just sit down and let me explain—"

"No. Not now." Not when she was so angry. And certainly not with him standing there without a shirt and looking so rumpled and sexy. "We'll talk, but not here and not now. I'm driving Belle's Suburban back to the ranch and I'm going to take a little time to think, then—"

"How much time?" he asked, fearing she might change her mind about talking to him.

"I'll call you in a couple of hours."

"C'mon, Rusty, we can talk it out. Just stay. Please."

The "please" took a chunk out of her resolve, but it held. "If you're afraid I'll run away, don't be. You're not getting off that easy." Calmly, head held high, she turned and went through the door, letting the screen bang shut behind her.

Logan knew a stonewall when he saw one. If he went after her now she would most likely tell him to drop dead and mean it. But he had allies. Quickly, he dialed the McBride Ranch.

"Hello."

"Belle, this is Logan—"

"You sound as sleepy as we are. In fact, we're still in bed."

"Could I, uh, talk to Cade?"

"Sure. Logan, is anything wrong?"

"Plenty. Paige is on her way to your house to return the Suburban, and she's—"

"Let me guess, y'all had a spat."

"It's more complicated than that, I'm afraid."

"Oh," Belle said. "Well, then, here's Cade."

"Hey, what's up?"

"My number if Paige has her way," Logan told him.

"She found out you're a P.I., huh? I tried to warn you."

"You can say 'I told you so' some other time. Right now, I need you to keep Paige at your place until I can get there."

"Do my best, but if she's hell-bent to leave I can't stop her."

"Don't I know. I'm on my way." He hung up

and took the stairs two at a time. He couldn't let her get away. He just couldn't.

BELLE WAS STANDING on the front porch when Paige drove up. She got out, walked up the steps and handed her the keys.

"I thought you should know Logan's on his way," Belle told her straight off.

"I figured as much."

"Would you like me to drive you somewhere? A motel? The airport?"

"Thanks, but no. I'm not leaving town just yet."

Belle smiled. "Good. Then could I interest you in a cup of coffee?"

Twenty minutes later Logan parked the Harley next to the Suburban and rang the McBrides' doorbell. Cade opened the door. "She's with Belle out on the patio, but I wouldn't recommend going out there."

"She's that mad?"

"I'm not talkin' about Paige. I'm talkin' about my wife."

"Belle?"

"Damn straight. She can be tougher than a rank bull when she gets mad. And I've been watching her get more ticked off by the minute. She's latched on to Paige like she's known her forever. Shea, too. You never should have brought her along if you were just messin' around—"

"I'm not. I mean, I was, but I'm not anymore."

Cade grinned. "Glad to hear it."

"You would be. That damned Fate of yours caught up with me."

Cade slapped him on the back. "Always does."

Logan walked through the house, opened the patio door and stepped out. Both women looked up at once, but it was Belle who rose and walked toward him. She opened her mouth to say something, then stopped, shook her head, then walked inside.

Logan approached Paige but didn't sit down in the chair next to her. He might not be here long enough to sit.

"I told you I would call you," she said.

"I know, but—"

"But you always have to do things your way. It doesn't matter." She looked up at him. "How long, Logan? How long have you known who I was?"

"Uh, almost from the first I knew you were running away from—"

"When we met on the road? When you rescued me?"

"Well, yeah. Sort of. I knew you'd given me a phony name and—"

"And all the time I thought you were so heroic, saving me from the bad guys. I fell into your hands like a ripe plum, didn't I? It couldn't have been any better if you'd planned it." She narrowed her gaze. "Or did you?"

"Listen, Rusty—"

"Don't call me that. Don't ever call me that again."

"No, I didn't plan to rescue you. But it didn't

take a rocket scientist to figure out you weren't a run-of-the-mill working girl."

"Yes, I remember your assessment of me. Tell me, were you working on my case before you left Denver or did you stumble across me and decide you had a gold mine?"

"My partner had taken the case before I left, but I didn't know any of the details."

"So, when you found out you had the Davenport heiress you decided to string my parents along for a few days to jack up your expenses?"

"Now wait just a damn minute. If you're implying what I think you're implying—"

"No, you wait." She thought she had her anger under control enough to tell him coolly and calmly what a louse he was, but she was wrong. All the rage and pain swirled into a ball inside her and exploded.

"I can't believe how gullible I was. You came riding up on that sleek, black motorcycle and I did everything but bat my eyelashes and say, 'My hero.' It makes me sick to my stomach to think how gullible I was. And how convenient that all my money was taken and you just happened to be able to make me a loan. And when I couldn't reach Regi you just took me in out of the kindness of your heart, right? Easy way to keep an eye on me, wasn't it?"

"Yeah, but not for the reasons you think."

"There's more? Oh, I can't wait to hear it."

"Aw, hell," he mumbled, knowing the truth was not going to win him any points.

"What was that?"

"I gave you money because you needed it.

And I admit I sort of pressured you into staying, but it wasn't to make sure you didn't run off.''

"Then why?"

"Because…" He propped a hand on his hip and, looking up, shook his head. She was going to have his hide, but it was better to get the truth out now. "Because I wanted to get you into bed."

"Excuse me?"

"You heard me. I wanted you. That's how it started, but—" He glanced down at her and couldn't finish his sentence. He'd never seen so much raw pain in anyone's eyes. He'd hurt her badly when that was the last thing in the world he wanted. Then, for a moment, just a second, a tiny flame of hope flared in his heart. She would have to care to be so hurt, wouldn't she? Maybe it was perverse logic, but he was hanging on by a thread.

"Paige, how did you find out I was a private detective?"

She blinked back tears. He wanted to get her into bed. He didn't love her. Her heart was lying in shreds at his feet and he wanted to know about logistics?

"I called my mother," she said, so softly he almost didn't hear her. "I told her she could call off the private investigators I knew she had searching for me," she told him, her voice growing stronger. "That's when I found out about Denver Investigations, Rick Conner and Logan Walker, owners."

"You told me you didn't want to contact your family. I thought your objective was to lead your own life."

"It is. But I don't have to stomp on others to do it. I simply realized that running away had been a childish thing to do. That no matter how they do, or don't, express it, my parents love me. What I did hurt them, and I had to apologize."

"So...all is forgiven? The prodigal can go home to open arms."

"I don't know about open arms, but yes, I think I can go home now without feeling trapped."

Go home now. Three little words that turned his world upside down. He crammed his hands in his pockets to keep from reaching for her, to keep from begging her not to leave. She'd made her choice and it wasn't him.

"So, I guess this is it, huh?"

Paige stared at him, unable to believe that this was the same man she had fallen in love with, the same man that had made love to her. She'd felt closer to him than any human being in her entire life. Now, he seemed light years away.

"Is that all you have to say, Logan? Not even an apology for what you've done?" What had she expected, him begging forgiveness followed by professions of undying love? That wasn't Logan Walker's style and he'd told her as much from the very beginning. Now she only had herself to blame.

She was convinced he'd only kept her with him because she was a case. He'd told her the truth and she hadn't believed him. What difference did it make? She was going back to her old life and he'd go back to his lonely one. "Would apologizing do any good?"

"I suppose not." She looked away, unable to bear seeing him so near yet forever out of her reach. Just end it, she thought. "Goodbye, Logan."

Love, desperate and deep, flooded him, nearly turning his legs boneless. He needed her. He didn't think he'd even suspected how much until this minute, and now it was too late. Now, he'd lost her.

"So long, Rusty." He turned and walked away. He walked through the house, out the front door to the bike, needing to get as far away from Paige, away from the pain, as he could.

"And just where the hell do you think you're going?"

Helmet in hand, Logan turned to find Belle standing a few feet away.

"I don't know," he said honestly. He couldn't bear the thought of going home without Paige.

"So, you lost round one. I sure didn't expect you to tuck your tail between your legs and head for the hills. Remember what Scarlett O'Hara said, 'Tomorrow is another day.'"

"Belle, I know you mean well, but I don't have the vaguest idea what you're talking about."

"I'm talking about you and Paige. You are coming back to talk to her after she's cooled down, aren't you? By tomorrow she'll be—"

"In Denver. And if she were any cooler, I'd have icicles hanging on my ears."

"What?"

"She's going home."

Belle put a hand on his shoulder, turning him

to face her, but he refused to look her in the eyes.
"Logan, do you love Paige?"

"What?"

"It's a simple question. Do you love Paige?"

"Yes."

"Did you tell her that?"

He scuffed the toe of his boot in the gravel in a
little boy gesture. "No."

Now she put both hands on her hips. "And
why not, may I ask?"

"Because she wants the kind of life she's always led."

"Bullshit!"

Logan's head snapped up. "Belle!" Tough as a
rank bull, Cade had said, and now he believed it.

"That's nothing compared to what I'd like to
say to you." She rolled her eyes. "And I thought
Cade was stubborn. What are you afraid of?"

"Afraid? I'm not—"

"Bull—"

"Okay." He cut her off. "I figured this would
happen. Sooner or later she would discover she
couldn't do without all that money and position
and she'd want to go back to it."

"You're right, that's not fear, it's just the usual
screwed-up male logic. But if logic does it for
you, try this. Paige isn't going home. She's staying in Reese's old cabin until her job in Houston
starts." At his stunned expression she smiled.
"And here's another little piece of logic for that
undersized male brain of yours. If Paige loved
money and the things it can buy so much, why
did she hock those expensive rocks she used to
wear in her ears so she could buy a new dress?

Couldn't be because she wanted you to be proud of her in front of your old classmates, could it? Couldn't be, knowing your resentment toward your ex-wife's selfishness, she wanted to be the polar opposite and do it on her own, could it?''

"She's not leaving?" Belle shook her head. "She hocked her diamond studs?" She nodded. "I had no idea."

"Men rarely do. But that's okay, we're not perfect either."

"Then, that must mean…" He looked at her, hope rising within him, and she smiled back. "…she loves me. And I love her."

"Don't tell me. Go tell her."

Logan grabbed Belle, literally lifting her off the ground, gave her a great big, smacking kiss, then set her down so fast she had to steady herself as he took off running toward the front door. He went past Cade in a blur.

"Great job, darlin'," Cade told his wife, having watched the whole thing from the front porch. "But if he ever kisses you again, I'll hafta get my gun."

"I think you should dust off your tux instead." She went up on her toes, looping her arms around his neck. "Looks like there's going to be a wedding."

Logan raced through the house, coming to a halt at the patio door. He took a deep breath and stepped outside. Paige was sitting exactly where he'd left her. "You're right," he said walking toward her. "I do owe you an apology."

Paige lifted her head and simply stared. "Go away, Logan."

"Can't do that."

"Then I will." She started to rise, but he stopped her with a hand on her shoulder. If he just hadn't touched her she would have been all right. Probably. But the feel of his hand on her shoulder went through her like a hot knife. The flood gates opened and she started to sob. "P-please, Logan. I c-can't t-take much m-more."

In a heartbeat he was beside her. "Don't cry, baby. Please, don't cry. I know you're hurt, but I swear to you that I didn't know who you were until yesterday. I even decided to resign and give the retainer back to your family. I didn't want you to think I hung on to you just because of my job. You've got to believe me. You've got to forgive me."

"No, I don't."

His hopes wobbled, but he was determined. "Yes, you do."

"Why?" she sniffed.

"Because I love you."

Paige stopped crying, looked at him. "You're asking me to believe that you didn't know your partner had signed on to search for me, and that we just happened to cross paths? And that you love me?"

"Yeah. It's this Fate thing that just seems to keep hitting me up beside the head until I get it."

"Fate thing?"

"A long time ago Cade told me that one of these days Fate would put a honey of a woman smack dab in the middle of my way, and it wouldn't make any difference if she had millions or pennies. I'd be a goner. And he was right."

"When?"

"When did he say it? Beats me if I can remember—"

"No, when did you start loving me?"

"I think I loved the idea of you before we even met, but I just never expected you to be real."

"Why not?"

"Maybe expected isn't the right word." He wiped away a few of the tears still glistening on her cheek. "I wasn't much more than a kid when I married Cindi, head over heels in love for the first time. When I found out what she was really like, what she really wanted, I told myself good riddance, the best thing was to avoid permanent relationships all together. And I surely did keep my word. But the truth is I was just plain scared to hang my heart out there and have it kicked to pieces again. It was just easier to blame it all on Cindi."

He offered a weak smile. "Then you came along and before I knew it you'd slipped right past that barrier straight into my heart. I wanted you from the first minute I saw those long, luscious legs of yours and I kept thinking that's all there was to it, but I couldn't keep you at a safe distance. You snuck up on my heart and before I knew it, I loved you."

He kissed her softly on the mouth. "I love you, Paige. You took a leap of faith with me once. Will you do it again? Forgive me? Marry me?"

She'd forgiven him the moment he said he loved her. "I should make you grovel. You know that, don't you?"

Thank God, she was going to forgive him. He slipped to his knees before her. "Is that a yes?"

"Yes," she whispered. "Yes, yes, yes. If you're sure you want a pain-in-the-ass rich girl like me?"

"Exactly like you." He started to kiss her again, stopped and drew back. "Uh, speaking of money, I, uh, think there's something you should know before I take you home, strip you naked and make mad passionate love to you."

"Tell me quick so we can get to the naked and passionate part."

"My dad's bottom line isn't quite up to Davenport standards, but I do have a healthy trust fund."

"You're rich?"

"Let's put it this way. I've got enough to help you start that art school for underprivileged kids and have enough left over to build us a house."

"But you already have a house that I love."

"It's in Sweetwater Springs. We both live in Denver. Never mind. We'll work it out. I don't care where we live just so long as we live together. So you'll marry me," he said again, "soon?"

"Yes," she repeated. "I guess I'll have to. I can't let you run around loose rescuing damsels in distress." She touched his cheek. "So, I better hang on to you. There just aren't enough heroes to go around these days."

Epilogue

"I DON'T KNOW how I let you talk me into this."
Logan handed Paige a magazine he'd bought for
her at one of the many newsstands in DFW Airport just before they boarded their flight for Denver.

"Because you love me?"

"I have a feeling that's going to get me into
more trouble over the next fifty or sixty years
than I ever expected."

Paige just smiled. "Probably."

"Just how big is this reception?" he asked.

"Oh…big." She didn't dare tell him four hundred invitations had been sent out or she'd never
get him out of her parents' house, much less to
the reception hall, despite the fact that all his
friends would be there too.

"And I guess you expect me to wear a tux?"

"Actually, I prefer you in nothing at all, but
I'm afraid my mother would never survive the
shock."

"Hey, I agreed not to ride the Harley up the
front steps of the mansion."

"I know. And, yes, you have to wear a tux."

When he groaned she leaned over and kissed
him. They had been joking around, but she knew
he was truly nervous about meeting her parents,
the reception and all of the fuss and bother that

went along with it. "Relax. Look at it this way.
You're only in for half of the usual misery."

"How's that?"

"Since we got married in front of a justice of
the peace, we skipped the ten bridesmaids and
groomsmen, fifty-foot veil and train, the drained
swimming pool full of gifts and the ceremony in
a fifteen-hundred-seat-capacity cathedral."

"Fifteen hundred?" He thought about that
number for a moment, then twisted in his seat to
face her. "Tell me that many haven't been in-
vited to this shindig your parents are throwing
for us? Please."

"Heavens, no. Not even half that number."
She started playing with the snaps on his Western-cut shirt, partly because she enjoyed it and
partly because it would distract him from thinking about the reception. Mostly because she just
loved to touch him. "Promise me something,
will you?" The quiet of the airplane was barely
disturbed by the sound of a snap popping.

"What's that? Uh, Rusty…"

"Promise me that you'll never wear anything
but these shirts." Another snap gave way and
she slipped her hand inside his shirt and sighed.
"They're just so…convenient."

"I'm going to give you two minutes to stop
that."

"Hmm." She loved his drawl, the sound of it
flowing over and through her like thick hot chocolate on the coldest day of the year.

"On second thought," he said when her fin-
gertip touched his nipple. "Better stop now. I
won't last that long." Besides he didn't want to

run the risk of her finding the small jeweler's box in his shirt pocket containing a pair of diamond studs. Larger than the ones she hocked, he thought proudly.

She leaned over and kissed the center of his chest.

"Rusty—"

"I'm just marking my place. For later."

Logan smiled, deciding this was the right time to bring up a problem they hadn't been able to find a reasonable solution for, no matter how reasonably they approach it. "You still like living in my grandmother's house?"

"Yes. We've been living there since we married a month ago and it feels like home. But I know you have your business, and since I do want to find a job in the arts, it just makes sense to live in Denver. More opportunities for both of us."

They wanted kids, lots of them. No lonely onlies for the Walkers. And they had talked about raising their children in Sweetwater Springs, but it would have to wait.

"Yeah, I guess. How do you think you would like to be the wife of the Chief of Police of Sweetwater Springs, Texas, population six hundred and three?"

"Tell him thank you for thinking of me, but I'm already married." She snuggled down in the seat and put her head on his shoulder.

"Rusty, I'm serious."

She sat up, looked at him. "What are you talking about?"

"Had a long conversation with Cade and Stan Hollingworth the other day."

"The mayor?"

"Yeah. They want to put my name before the town council for chief of police. The pay's not great, but we could live in the house."

"And you could get killed," she said.

"I probably stand a greater chance of being in an auto accident in Denver than killed in Sweetwater Springs."

Okay, she'd give him that, but she wasn't sure she liked the idea of him being a cop again. "I have to admit I like that part. And it would mean we could start a family sooner."

"Yeah." He grinned. "And I like that part."

"Still..." She snuggled back down. "I don't mind you being my hero, but I'm not sure I want you to make a career out of it. Can we think about it? It's our whole future, you know."

With one hand, he tucked the love of his life securely to his side. "Absolutely," he said, tenderly kissing the top of her head. From where he sat the future looked downright spectacular.

This month's
irresistible novels from

TEMPTATION®

ALWAYS A HERO by Kate Hoffmann

Isabelle Channing wants to save her friend from marrying the wrong man but somehow ends up with the prospective groom herself! One minute she is stuck in a lift with upright yet sexy as hell Colin and a bottle of bubbly on New Year's Eve, and the next thing Isabelle knows, she is a married woman...

TANGLED SHEETS by Jo Leigh

The Wrong Bed

Maggie Beaumont is ready to seduce her fianc . She never suspects for a moment that the man she sneaks off with, away from the masquerade party, is her ex-husband Spencer Daniels. What now? The sheets are tangled and Maggie is left with the thrill of Spencer's touch blazing in her mind...

UNLIKELY HERO by Sandy Steen

Feisty redhead Paige Davenport takes her life in her hands when she runs away from her wedding. So when her car breaks down she's lucky that sexy private eye Logan Walker comes along. He's spotted she's in trouble and before long, so is he—all he can think of is keeping her in his bed...

JUST FOR THE NIGHT by Leandra Logan

Bachelor Auction

Millionaire bachelor Garrett McNamara is for sale for charity. Waitress Shari Johnson's been fantasising about him since their school days, waiting for just one chance to get close to him, get him out of her head. Trouble is, the more she's with him, the more she wants him...

Spoil yourself next month
with these four novels from

TEMPTATION®

CLUB CUPID by Stephanie Bond

Frankie Jensen hadn't planned to be stranded in Florida on
Valentine's Day with sinfully sexy Randy Tate. But the
gorgeous bar owner tempted her to let go and indulge in a few
fantasies…

TALL, DARK AND RECKLESS by Lyn Ellis

Mail Order Men

Lawman Matt Travis thrives on the unexpected—until he's
surrounded by a group of sex-starved women! Even the local
TV station has been called! And when sexy journalist Dee Cates
saunters up to him, Matt finds himself up against a truly
powerful adversary: desire…

BLACK VELVET VALENTINES by Carrie Alexander

Blaze (3 short stories)

Secrets of the Heart: Somebody's sending Charlotte Colfax
black velvet valentines—but who? *Two Hearts:* Pansy
Kingsmith has a plan—but when twins are involved there's
bound to be a mix up! *Heart's Desire:* Angie Dubonnet never
expected her cruise would be such a voyage of sensual
discovery…

SAY 'AHHH…' by Donna Sterling

Back from the city, Dr Connor Wade wanted an uncomplicated
country girl to settle down with. Imagine his surprise when into
his surgery walked Sarah Flowers—not uncomplicated, but
everything he'd ever wanted in a woman…

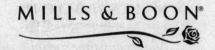

2 FREE

books and a surprise gift!

We would like to take this opportunity to thank you for reading this Mills & Boon® book by offering you the chance to take TWO more specially selected titles from the Temptation® series absolutely FREE! We're also making this offer to introduce you to the benefits of the Reader Service™—

★ FREE home delivery
★ FREE gifts and competitions
★ FREE monthly Newsletter
★ Exclusive Reader Service discounts
★ Books available before they're in the shops

Accepting these FREE books and gift places you under no obligation to buy, you may cancel at any time, even after receiving your free shipment. Simply complete your details below and return the entire page to the address below. *You don't even need a stamp!*

YES! Please send me 2 free Temptation books and a surprise gift. I understand that unless you hear from me, I will receive 4 superb new titles every month for just £2.40 each, postage and packing free. I am under no obligation to purchase any books and may cancel my subscription at any time. The free books and gift will be mine to keep in any case.

T0EA

Ms/Mrs/Miss/Mr ....Initials.....................................
                                         BLOCK CAPITALS PLEASE

Surname ....

Address ....

....

....Postcode..................................

Send this whole page to:
UK: FREEPOST CN81, Croydon, CR9 3WZ
EIRE: PO Box 4546, Kilcock, County Kildare (stamp required)

MARY LYNN BAXTER

ONE SUMMER EVENING

she could never forget...

Cassie has been living a nightmare since
she left her parents' luxurious home
nine years ago after a reckless act of love
changed her life forever. Now she believes
she's safe and has returned...
but danger has followed her.

Published 21st January 2000

**Available from all good
paperback stockists.**